R0068693423

11/2013

MOZAMBIQUE

SWAZILAND

INDIAN OCEAN

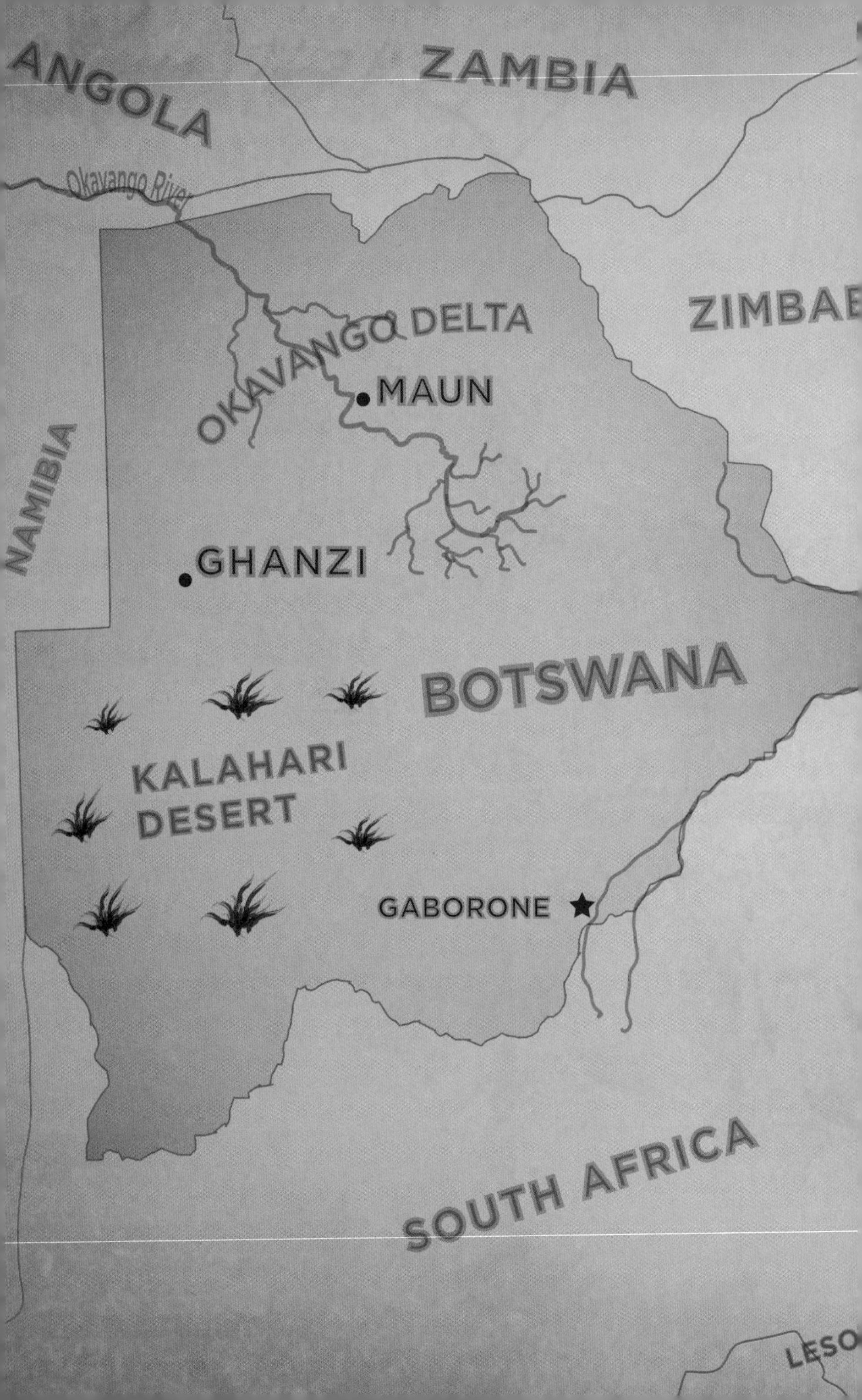

ANGOLA
ZAMBIA
Okavango River
ZIMBAB
OKAVANGO DELTA
MAUN
NAMIBIA
GHANZI
BOTSWANA
KALAHARI
DESERT
GABORONE
SOUTH AFRICA
LESO

TRAVELS WITH **GANNON & WYATT**

# BOTSWANA

## PATTI WHEELER & KEITH HEMSTREET

GREENLEAF
BOOK GROUP PRESS

Published by Greenleaf Book Group Press
Austin, Texas
www.gbgpress.com

Distributed by Greenleaf Book Group LLC
For ordering information or special discounts for bulk purchases, please contact Greenleaf Book Group LLC at PO Box 91869, Austin, TX 78709, 512.891.6100.

Design and composition by Greenleaf Book Group LLC
Cover design and illustration by Leon Godwin

Cataloging-in-Publication data
(Prepared by The Donohue Group, Inc.)
Wheeler, Patti.
    Travels with Gannon & Wyatt. Botswana / Patti Wheeler & Keith Hemstreet.—2nd ed.
    p. : ill. ; cm.
    Originally published: Aspen, CO : Claimstake Productions, 2010.
    Summary: Twin explorers Gannon and Wyatt go to Botswana for an African safari, but a poacher has shot and wounded a lioness, and as they set off to try to save the mother and her cubs, they encounter many of Africa's big animals. Based on real-life brothers, this series is supported by video, photos, and more stories found online at travelswithgannonandwyatt.com.
    Interest age level: 009-012.
    Issued also as an ebook.
    ISBN: 978-1-60832-585-6

    1. Twins—Juvenile fiction. 2. Poaching—Botswana—Juvenile fiction. 3. Game protection—Botswana—Juvenile fiction. 4. Adventure and adventurers—Botswana—Juvenile fiction. 5. Botswana—Juvenile fiction. 6. Twins—Fiction. 7. Poaching—Botswana—Fiction. 8. Game protection—Botswana—Fiction. 9. Adventure and adventurers—Botswana—Fiction. 10. Botswana—Fiction. 11. Adventure stories. 12. Diary fiction. I. Hemstreet, Keith. II. Title. III. Title: Travels with Gannon and Wyatt. IV. Title: Botswana
PZ7.W5663 Bot 2013
[Fic]                                                        2013933149

Part of the Tree Neutral® program, which offsets the number of trees consumed in the production and printing of this book by taking proactive steps, such as planting trees in direct proportion to the number of trees used: www.treeneutral.com

Printed in the United States of America on acid-free paper
13 14 15 16 17 18   10 9 8 7 6 5 4 3 2 1
Second Edition

Travel is fatal to prejudice, bigotry,
and narrow-mindedness.

—Mark Twain


Do not follow where the path may lead.
Go instead where there is no path and leave a trail.

—Ralph Waldo Emerson

## ENGLISH/SETSWANA:
TRANSLATION OF COMMON PHRASES

**Hello, Sir/Madam**—Dumela, rra/mma

**How are you?**—O kae?

**I am fine**—Ke teng

**What is your name?**—Leina la gago ke mang?

**My name is . . .** —Leina la me ke . . .

**Where are you from?**—O tswakae?

**Please**—Tswee-tswee

**Thank you, Sir/Madam**—Ke a leboga, rra/mma

**I'm hungry**—Ke tshwerwe ke tlala

**I'm thirsty**—Ke tshwerwe ke lenyora

**I like**—Ke rata

**I don't like**—Ga ke rate

**Where is the hospital?**—Kokelwana e ko kae?

**I need help, please**—Ke kopa thuso, tswee-tswee

**May I help you?**—A nka go thusa?

**Goodbye**—Tsamaya sentle

# CONTENTS

# PART I

## JOURNEY TO
## THE DARK CONTINENT

# WYATT

**B**y mid-morning tomorrow, we'll be aboard a plane, flying in an easterly direction, probably somewhere over Colorado still, but en route to a far-off land . . . Africa!

Just say the word "Africa" and all sorts of wild images are brought to mind—elephants stampeding across the savannah, yipping baboons swinging from the limbs of trees, hippos and crocodiles lurking just under the water's surface, an elusive leopard silently stalking a herd of antelope, a pride of hungry lions devouring a fresh kill, tribesmen stepping cautiously through the bush on the hunt for their next meal.

Africa is one of a kind. Untamed. Exotic. Mysterious. Bigger than big. When you think about it, Africa is not so much a continent as it is a world of its own.

In the field of scientific exploration, one of the last

remaining places on earth to be studied was the African interior. For centuries, the outside world knew little about it, except that it was full of dangers that could bring an expedition to an abrupt and tragic end. Africa was such a mystery, in fact, that the great explorers of the 1800s labeled it the "dark continent." For this reason, they were determined to shed some light on Africa, to march into the bush and see with their own eyes what this mysterious world was really like. Over the next century, many explorers became famous for leading scientific expeditions into this uncharted territory. Some lived to tell about it. Many did not.

Reading the journals of these brave explorers gave me the idea of keeping my own journal during our upcoming adventure. When I mentioned it to my mom, she thought it was such a good idea that she incorporated it into our home-school curriculum. Gannon and I went to the bookstore and each bought a leather-bound journal, just like the famous explorers used on their expeditions. These books will be dedicated specifically to our daily record, or "field notes," as I like to call them. Our field notes will also serve another important purpose. When we return from Africa, we're going to submit them to the Youth Exploration Society (Y.E.S.), an organization of explorers whose mission is to inform young people of ways to help cultures, species, and environments at risk. If they are worthy, and we're going to do our best to make sure they are, they will be housed in the Y.E.S. library right alongside some of the most famous books of exploration ever published.

Visiting Africa has been a dream of mine for as long as I can remember, and tomorrow we'll be on our way! I still have a lot of packing to do, but before closing my first journal entry I want to make a note on how this adventure came about. It had been a while since our last trip and we were itching to begin another journey. One night over dinner, we talked about our options. Given my mom's job at World Airlines, our family can fly almost anywhere for free, so long as there are seats available. So, she made a few calls, jotted down a list of the destinations available and told us all to write our choice on a small piece of paper. She gathered our votes and read them aloud. Amazingly, we'd all chosen the same place: Botswana!

# GANNON

Turbulence!

Oh, man, it really turns my stomach. We must be passing through a huge thunderstorm because right now it feels like this plane is driving over a never-ending dirt road full of potholes. Out the window all I see is darkness and the flashing red light on the tip of the wing and all these clouds streaking past like some kind of crazy ghosts flying at Mach speed in the opposite direction.

This is probably the worst time to start my journal because my handwriting is all over the place and my mom won't be too happy about that when she grades my penmanship and I'll have to explain to her that it was because the plane was bouncing all over the sky, but right now I have to do something to try to take my mind off this bumpy ride and journaling seems to be the best option.

According to Wyatt, it's about seventeen hours from the time you take off in Washington, D.C., to the time you land in Johannesburg, South Africa. That's where we will switch planes and fly to Botswana, which will take another couple hours, I think. We're about fourteen hours into the flight and still somewhere over the Atlantic Ocean.

Okay, now this is more like it. I think we've made it through the storm. At least the plane isn't getting knocked around anymore, and thank goodness for that, because I was about to put the old barf bag to good use, if you know what I mean.

The sun is just now coming up and painting the sky in all these amazing colors. It looks like some kind of abstract artwork where the artist takes out a brush and paints patterns or shapes in all kinds of bright shades. My dad has done some paintings like that—the abstract kind—and I really like them, but he focuses mostly on wildlife and landscape paintings. Can't wait to see what sort of paintings he makes in Botswana.

Since leaving D.C., I don't think I've slept more than three, maybe four hours tops, but I feel really alert. It might have something to do with all the soda I've had on this flight or that awful turbulence, but I think it's mostly due to our destination. In all of our travels, I don't know that I've ever been so amped about a trip.

I think Wyatt's even more excited than I am, if that's possible. The kid can't keep his mouth shut. He's been babbling on through the night about all sorts of things that— to be completely honest—I could care less about, like the digestive system of a giraffe and the monsoons that flood the Okavango Delta every year and all this other stuff I totally tuned out. I mean, the kid thinks he's Charles Darwin reincarnated or something. How twins could be so different is totally baffling to me. I guess some people get into all of that stuff, but not me. Science bores me to tears. I'm not saying it isn't important or anything. Of course it's important. It's just that learning how many hours a day an elephant spends eating grass or how to navigate through the bush using the stars doesn't bring me to the edge of my seat with excitement.

So that's not the kind of stuff I'm going to write about in my journal. I'd rather write about the things I experience while traveling—the things that leave a lasting impression on me. Now, I'm not trying to be all profound or philosophical or anything, but if you get all wrapped up in the details of things, like my obsessive-compulsive brother, well, sometimes you miss what's really important. A welcoming smile from a child in a foreign city, for example. Or the affectionate nudge a mama bear gives her cub. I like to spend some time thinking about these things, and not just take them for what they appear to be on the surface—a child smiling or a bear nudging its cub—but really wonder to myself what these things mean. Like, what thoughts are running through their mind at that very moment? Maybe I'll write about that stuff. To me, that is what's really fascinating. That's life!

Of course, this is just my opinion. Everyone sees things differently. I bet if you sent ten people on the same trip, you'd probably hear ten different stories when they got back. Everyone has different interests and different opinions about things. My brother and I are no different.

It's funny, or sad (depends how you look at it, I guess), but when I told my friends back in Colorado that we were going to Africa, almost everyone asked, "Why?" It made me wonder if my friends would ever venture beyond their own backyards. I mean, who asks "why" about the chance to travel? I say, "Why not?" Why not expand your horizons? Why not learn about new cultures? Why not see what there is beyond your home turf?

I guess we're lucky. I mean, with a flight attendant for a mom and an artist for a dad, we're pretty much a bunch of nomads, always hopping around the globe from one amazing place to the next, and I have to say, I absolutely love being a nomad!

Looking out my window, I notice that we're over land. Wyatt tells me that the country of Namibia is directly below us. The early morning sun lights the barren desert landscape. Other than long dirt roads that disappear into the haze, there are no signs of anything man-made. No cities, no towns. No trees or water either. Just parched land, as far as the eye can see.

Wow, it's almost hard to believe.

Africa!

## WYATT

AUGUST 21, 12:24 PM
MAUN, BOTSWANA, 19° 58′ S 23° 25′ E
21° CELSIUS, 70° FAHRENHEIT
SKIES CLEAR, WIND CALM


Just before 11:00 a.m., we landed in Maun, a dusty town of about 50,000 people in north-central Botswana. I am sitting on the steps outside the airport. A man just walked up and asked if I wanted to buy any bananas. I looked into the man's bag, thinking that a banana might actually hit the spot and provide a good dose of potassium to help keep my muscles working properly, but the bananas were all too ripe and bruised. Maybe that's the way they like to eat them here, but there wasn't one in the bunch that looked appetizing to me. Politely, I said, "No, thank you," and the man moved on.

We are waiting for a connecting flight to our camp in the Kalahari Desert, which is about an hour away. We'll be flying on a small plane. That would scare some people, but I love small planes. When you're in a small plane you really get the sensation of flying, of moving through the sky from one point to another. Whereas in a jumbo jet, you more or less feel like you're in a movie theater or something. When we landed in Maun I took a look in the hangar and saw a few Caravans, which seat eleven or twelve people, and even a couple Cessna 206s, which only seat six, including the pilot. Both are single-engine planes and very reliable.

Tomorrow we will begin our safari. First, we'll explore parts of the Kalahari Desert, a stretch of dunes and salt pans, which covers over 100,000 square miles in Botswana, Namibia and South Africa. We'll live in tents near a Bushmen village and attempt to track the great white rhino. After a week in the Kalahari, we will fly to the Okavango Delta, a system of inland waterways and islands. Monsoon rains flood the delta each year, and where there is water, there is wildlife! Having the chance to go into the African bush and observe the wildlife in an environment that has hardly changed in thousands of years, that's every budding scientist's dream. And now, just a short thirty hours after leaving Denver International Airport, I am here! It's really amazing to think that just yesterday I was having breakfast in North America, and now I'm in Africa. It's like my mom always says, "Any place in the world, no matter how far, is just a few flights away."

As I write this, I'm watching my brother walk aimlessly down the sidewalk, stopping to talk to random people. It's anybody's guess what he's asking these people. With his blond hair and blue eyes, the kid sticks out like a sore thumb. I guess I do, too. But sticking out never seems to faze Gannon. I have to admit, I don't know anyone else who can strike up conversations with total strangers like my brother does. He's a real people person.

## GANNON
TUESDAY, I THINK . . . MAYBE WEDNESDAY

After we got to Maun and got our passports stamped, there was still some time before we were scheduled to fly to the Kalahari, so I did what I normally do when I get to a new place—I walked around and talked to the locals. Whenever I do this, I try to say something in the native language because I feel that doing so shows you respect the local culture. Now, I'll admit, not everybody I come across is totally receptive to this kind of thing. Truth is, you never really know how someone is going react when a perfect stranger walks up and says, "Hello!" Like, for example, when I was in Russia and I did this, not many people said hello back. They usually just walked by without a glance or if they did look at me it was one of those cockeyed looks like I was some kind of crazy kid who should be locked up in a funny farm. Come to think of it, a lot of people in New York City acted the same way, so maybe it's a big-city thing, not just a Russian thing. Well, whatever it is, I think friendliness can be understood anywhere, by anyone. Whether people say hello back or not, I'm pretty sure that they will remember me at some point and say, "You know, that boy who said 'hello' to me that day was real friendly. If everyone was as friendly as that boy I bet the world would be a much better place." At least, that's what I like to think.

Exploring Maun was really interesting. I had my video camera in hand and was taking some footage of the people and the storefronts and this random donkey that was walking all alone down the middle of the road when I came across an older man seated behind a small booth just off the sidewalk. I greeted him using some Setswana words that I'd studied on the plane. Setswana, other than English, is the official language of Botswana.

"Hallo," I said to the man. "Leina la me ke, Gannon. Ketswako United States. O bua Sekhowa?"

Translation to English: "Hello. My name is Gannon. I'm from the United States. Do you speak English?"

"A little," he said, nodding his head.

He was nice enough to offer me a chair and with his permission I filmed a little bit of our conversation. He spoke better English than he gave himself credit for and went on to tell me how he was born in Maun and had lived there his whole life, but that he wasn't born in a hospital like me, he was born in a hut that his father had built from mud, sticks and tree branches. The floor of the hut was mostly dirt, but in one area there was a small rug that his mother had knitted and she delivered him right there, on that rug! His brother and sister were born on the rug, too. I can't even imagine!

He talked about how he'd seen Maun grow from a tiny village of mud huts to the sprawling town it is today with all kinds of concrete office buildings, restaurants, shops, gas stations, and other little businesses. He said the town had grown mostly because safaris were bringing more and more visitors to Maun every year.

The man spent most days at his booth selling wooden sculptures that he and his wife carve with their own hands. This man had never gone to school to learn how to carve wood and neither had his wife—they taught themselves how to do it through years and years of practice. Judging by the quality of their artwork I would have guessed that they had been taught at a school for sculptors in Paris or Rome or wherever the best sculptors are taught. I'm not joking, they were that good!

I ended up buying a small wooden elephant for my cousin Bliss. She's five years old and loves big animals, especially elephants. I didn't have any local currency, but the man said he would gladly accept US money and charged me two dollars. Now, I don't know much about valuing art, but two dollars seemed like an amazing deal for this sculpture. I thanked the man the best I could in Setswana: "Ke a leboga." He just chuckled and nodded, partly as thanks for my purchase and partly, I'm guessing, because I butchered his language.

As I walked back to the airport, happy to have met this friendly sculptor and learned a little bit about what life is like in Maun, I noticed a rusty old jeep parked on the side of the road. As I came closer, I saw a man putting several rifles in the back, the hunting kind, with scopes attached to the top and all. There are certain people who—just by looking at them—bring about an uneasy feeling in the pit of my stomach. Well, this guy was definitely one of those people. He wore a beat-up safari hat and his shirt and pants were torn in places and filthy with dirt and who knows what else and there was a patch over his left eye, just like a pirate. But it wasn't so much the eye patch that gave me the creeps. What really creeped me out was the man's good eye. It was completely black, like a marble. I'm not joking, there was no color whatsoever. It was just a deep, dark hole.

Passing the jeep, the man turned and glared at me and when our eyes met this crazy chill went shooting down my spine. How he could see anything out of that black eye, I have no idea, but he could see, that's for sure. I could tell just by the way he stared at me. I looked away and picked up my pace, double-timing it to the airport without ever looking back. Maun was well worth a quick stop, but I'm definitely ready to get on with the safari.

## WYATT

AUGUST 21, 7:34 PM
KALAHARI DESERT, 21° 29′ S 21° 50′ E
19° CELSIUS, 66° FAHRENHEIT
ELEVATION: 3,780 FEET
SKIES CLEAR

We flew to camp in a Cessna 206, like I had hoped. After working so many years for the airlines, my mom should be comfortable on just about any type of plane, but she was as scared as a little kid on a rickety old roller coaster.

When she first saw the plane, her eyes got really wide. "Is this our plane?" she asked. "Please tell me this is not our plane." When she found out it was, in fact, our plane, she turned white as snow.

Soon after the pilot started the engine, my mom began

sniffing the air like a dog does when it's looking for food. "Does anyone smell smoke?" she said. "I smell smoke. Something is burning!"

No one else smelled smoke. I think it was all in her imagination.

The Cessna 206 that flew us to the Kalahari

As the plane lifted off, it was bounced around by a stiff wind. I really thought my mom might faint. My dad laughed out loud at the sight of my mom, who had her eyes closed and a white-knuckle grip on the armrests. Maybe it was the pilot, who looked like he was barely eighteen years old, or maybe it was the toylike size of the plane, or maybe it was a fear that flight regulations in Botswana aren't as strict as they are in other parts of the world. Whatever it was, my mom was terrified.

With four passengers plus baggage, the Cessna 206 was literally packed from floor to ceiling, but somehow we all managed to fit. Before we boarded I challenged Gannon to a game of rock-paper-scissors for the copilot's seat.

"Bring it on," he said.

"One, two, three," I said, as we pounded our fists into our palms.

I took Gannon the first two games—rock over scissors, paper over rock.

"Could be a sweep," I said.

"Won't happen," Gannon said confidently.

He was right. He came charging back and tied it up 2–2.

"This is for the win," he said. "So, I'm going to tell you straight up. I'm going with rock."

"Whatever," I said.

"Don't say I didn't warn you."

Typically, when Gannon tells me what he is going to throw, he sticks with it. It's his way of messing with my head. Then, if he wins, he gets to say, "I told you what I was going to throw and I still beat you!"

"One, two, three," I said, and threw paper, expecting him to stick with rock, as he said. Of course, he threw scissors.

"Oh, that's too bad," Gannon said, laughing.

"Best out of seven?" I asked.

"No thanks," he said and climbed up front.

I was totally bummed because sitting up front makes you feel like you are actually flying the plane. But even sitting in back with my backpack on my lap, I enjoyed the flight. According to the altimeter, we were cruising between 4,900 and 5,000 feet above sea level, which, given the elevation of the Kalahari, put us about 1,200 feet off the ground. Just low enough to get a great view of the desert.

View of the Cessna dashboard

During the flight, we passed over several brush fires. At times the air was so hazy you couldn't even see the ground. The pilot told us that fires often start when lightning strikes the dry brush, but that lately poachers have been starting fires in order to trap animals and make it easier to hunt them.

Poachers are people who illegally hunt animals for their valuable skins, furs, ivory tusks, horns, etc. Poachers pose a great threat to the wildlife, since the more animals they kill, the more money they make. I could only hope that the fires we saw were started by lightning.

We landed on a small dirt airstrip in the western Kalahari. From the airstrip we were driven over bumpy dirt roads, kicking up huge clouds of dust as we weaved our way through the desert brush. Yellow flowers budded on thorny acacia bushes. The leaves of umbrella trees made circles of shade on the sand. We even saw a kudu peek its head out from behind a shrub. As we neared the camp, the sun was falling. The sky turned bright red and the air blowing through the jeep was cool.

Edo's Camp is a cluster of tents that will serve as our home for the next week. When we arrived, our guide, Chocs, and his daughter, Jubjub, greeted us. A native of Botswana, Chocs is tall and strong, with the most perfect white teeth I've ever seen. Chocs had gone to a university in England and earned a degree in environmental science and zoology. When he got back to Botswana, he started a safari business.

Jubjub was born and raised in the bush. Because her father's work kept them traveling back and forth between the Kalahari and the Okavango Delta, Jubjub was homeschooled just like us. Her mother, whom Chocs had met when they were both children, manages the family's safari business.

Jubjub seemed very confident and mature, which I guess is inevitable when you grow up in an environment as wild as this. When Gannon told her that he liked her name, she told us that Jubjub means "savior."

We all gathered around the fire pit underneath a sprawling camel thorn tree. A dozen or so wildebeest drank from the watering hole, along with a group of waterbuck and a big male kudu. As the last light faded, a million stars appeared in the desert sky.

"I'd like to welcome you all to Botswana and the great Kalahari Desert," Chocs said with a big smile. "There are only a handful of places left in the world where you can enjoy nature in its pristine state. The Kalahari Desert and Okavango Delta are two such places. While in Botswana, you will encounter all of the Big Five. Does anyone know what animals make up the Big Five?"

Gannon raised his hand, and Chocs pointed to him.

"Lions, elephants, leopards, Cape buffalo, and . . . uh . . . the hippo?"

"Close," Chocs said. "You were correct with the exception of the hippo. It's the rhino, not the hippo, that is part of the Big Five. Speaking of rhinos, have a look."

Chocs pointed to the far end of the watering hole. A large white rhino was coming out of the brush. It walked slowly to the edge of the pond, lowered its head and took a drink.

"Next to the elephant," Chocs said, "the white rhino is the largest land-bound mammal on Earth."

"What a beautiful animal," my father said. "They are so prehistoric. I can't wait to get to work."

My father's job while we're in Botswana is to photograph and make paintings of the white rhino. When we return home he's going to create a life-size sculpture of this rare animal for an art collector in Santa Fe, New Mexico.

"Does anyone have any questions before we move to the dining tent?" Chocs asked.

"I do," Gannon said.

"Yes?"

"Are there any spiders out here?" Gannon asked.

"Yes, big ones," Chocs replied with a wide grin on his face. "But we don't make you pay extra for them."

Gannon looked at me and smiled, knowing how much I hate spiders. I took a deep breath and tried my best not to think about it.

Jubjub walked down from the kitchen. "Excuse me," she said. "The wildebeest stew is ready."

Was she serious? Wildebeest stew? Just the sound of it made my stomach feel uneasy. Then again, you never know whether or not you'll like something until you try it. While traveling, I stick to the rationale that if the food is good enough for the locals, it's good enough for me. That doesn't always mean that I'll like it, but at least I'll give it a try.

"If we can all follow Jubjub to the dining tent," Chocs

said, "we've prepared a wonderful African meal for you. I hope you are all ready for an adventure, because an adventure is what we have in store."

## GANNON

AUGUST 22
EARLY MORNING

Last night, after a small bowl of wildebeest stew—it was okay, but a little too gamey for my taste—I walked back to our tent under a starlit sky and fell asleep before my head hit the pillow. I was so tired I don't think I would have woken up if a rhino had walked up and licked my face.

It's still winter here in the southern hemisphere. I didn't really think of Africa as being a place that got cold, especially the desert, but it actually gets super cold here in the Kalahari. So cold that Chocs gave each of us a hot water bottle to keep under our down blankets during the night, and thank goodness for that, because I left the window flap open and woke in the middle of the night to all this wind blowing inside the tent, but I was just too tired to get out of bed and zip it up and probably would have turned into a human popsicle if it hadn't been for that warm water bottle. This morning I put on just about every piece of clothing I brought with me— long pants, a long-sleeved T-shirt, a fleece sweater, a winter jacket, and a wool beanie cap—and even bundled up in all these clothes, I can't stop shivering. Wyatt's thermometer reads 37 degrees Fahrenheit and factoring in the wind chill I'm guessing it's way below freezing.

I've already checked my equipment several times this morning to make quadruple sure my video camera is in good working order. There's nothing more frustrating than getting out in the field and realizing your camera batteries are all dead. I've learned that the hard way. But no more bonehead mistakes from this kid. If I want to be a filmmaker when I get older I have to go about it like a professional, and right now I can't think of anything I'd rather do than make films that teach people about the world and how big and different it can be from place to place and at the same time how we're all really similar in so many ways. That's the ironic thing, I guess. No matter how different we seem to be, when you really break it down, we're all very much alike. Sure, we may not look alike and we might speak different languages and have different customs and beliefs and live in different kinds of homes and do different things for work, but most of us share the same kinds of thoughts and hopes and dreams.

It'll be really interesting to learn more about the Bushmen. I mean, their culture is about as different from ours as you can get. Right after breakfast, Chocs and Jubjub will be taking us to their village. Jubjub told us that traditionally the Bushmen are hunter-gatherers, which means they hunt and gather food from the land. She said they've been living this way for tens of thousands of years, but as people buy up more and more land around them the areas where they can hunt get smaller, so most Bushmen have actually given up hunting and become farmers since that is the only way they can provide enough food for their families.

What a privilege it will be to meet them. I mean, how many people get the chance to hang out with the Bushmen of the Kalahari? Forget breakfast, I'm ready to go now! Then again, I am a little numb from this frigid desert air. Maybe it's a better idea to go warm up by the fire pit and let the sun burn off some of this cold before we go speeding off in a topless jeep. Yeah, definitely a better plan.

Gannon, out.

## WYATT

AUGUST 22, 11:22 AM
KALAHARI DESERT
16° CELSIUS, 60° FAHRENHEIT
SKIES CLEAR

When Chocs warned us that we had an adventure in store, I doubt he had what happened this morning in mind.

On our way to the Bushmen village, my mom spotted something moving through the acacia trees about fifty yards from the road.

"Stop the jeep!" she yelled, pointing. "I just saw something! And it was big!"

Chocs stopped the jeep and looked through his binoculars. In the distance, he spotted a family of white rhinos casually walking through the bushes.

"A male, a female, and two babies," he said. "And they're coming this way. I'm going to turn off the jeep so we don't frighten them."

Jubjub took the binoculars from her father and looked at the rhinos.

"That's the pregnant mother we saw last month," she said. "She had her babies. They can't be more than a few weeks old."

The jeep didn't have a roof, so we all stood up for a better look. Sure enough, a family of rhinos was coming right toward us. When they came within a hundred feet or so, they stopped, as if they had suddenly sensed that we were near.

The female rhino at a safe distance, or so I thought

"Rhinos have very poor eyesight," Chocs whispered. "But they definitely know we're here."

White rhinos aren't actually white; they're gray, with two horns on the bridge of their snout. The horn closest to their nostrils is about three times the size of the other horn. Their bodies are so massive it seems impossible that their small, stubby legs could carry them. Their eyes are like black pinballs, and their ears are twisted like conch shells.

The rhino family stood very still for a while, as if they were confused about what to do next. Watching them in awe, I had a false sense of security, like I was watching them from behind a high cement wall at the zoo. But that sense of security vanished the instant one of the babies started trotting our way.

Chocs immediately sprang to his feet, clapping his hands and yelling in an attempt to make the baby turn in a different direction. But the baby continued, jogging right up to the jeep like a puppy looking for a playmate. The second baby followed close behind.

"No!" Chocs yelled. "Go back! Go!"

"Turn around!" Jubjub yelled. "Go back to your mother and father!"

The male and female rhinos were getting angry, jerking their heads around and huffing loudly. When one of the babies disappeared behind the jeep, the female rhino charged.

Chocs dropped into the driver's seat and tried to start the jeep, but the engine sputtered and stalled.

"Everyone hold on tight!" Chocs yelled.

I put my camera down and grabbed on to the roll bar. The ground rumbled, and we all braced for impact, as this giant of the Kalahari thundered toward us. Right up to the last second, I doubted the rhino would actually ram the jeep, assuming she somehow understood that doing so would hurt her more than it hurt the vehicle. Boy, was I wrong.

There was a deafening sound, like two cars colliding at high speed, as the rhino slammed into the jeep. The vehicle tilted and almost rolled over on its side. My mom lost her grip and fell out the back, landing hard on the ground.

"Mom!" Gannon yelled. He reached out to help her back into the jeep, but the female rhino cut her off before she could climb inside. My mom backed up facing the rhino, her eyes wide with fear. The rhino glared at her and lifted its sharp horn in quick jerks, as if warning my mom that she wasn't afraid to use it. My dad jumped out of the jeep and ran to my mom. The male rhino soon joined the attack, swiping hard at the jeep with the side of his head while he circled around us. This constant ramming of the jeep startled the babies, and eventually they ran off into the bushes. The male rhino quickly followed. But the female stood her ground, facing off with my mom and dad. She looked like she was ready to charge at any moment.

Chocs stepped from the jeep and moved slowly toward my parents.

"Everyone talk loudly now!" he said. "Should the rhino charge, run behind that tree to your left! Do you see it?"

"Yes," my mom said, her voice shaking. "I see it."

"Okay, good!" Chocs said. "Now let's everyone continue to talk loudly!"

Everyone followed his instructions.

"We're all talking loudly to the rhinos!" Jubjub said.

"Yes, we're all talking loudly!" my dad echoed.

"Talk loudly, Wyatt!" Gannon said.

Everything was happening so fast, I hadn't realized that I was just standing there, silent as a mouse.

"Okay, Gannon! I'm talking loudly now! Talking loudly to the rhinos!"

All of the voices seemed to startle the rhino. She took a few steps back and looked around frantically, as if trying to spot her family.

"That's good!" Chocs continued. "She's moving back! Everyone continue to talk loudly!"

"We're talking loudly!" I said. "Talking loudly! Talking loudly!"

It felt awkward, all of us talking loudly to a rhino, but it worked. The female rhino eventually turned and ran off, disappearing into the bushes behind a billowing cloud of dust.

My mother was so shaken she could hardly speak. Her entire body was trembling. Chocs and my dad helped her back into the truck. Once she was safely inside, Gannon and I hugged and kissed her as if we hadn't seen her in years. She'd just cheated death, and it would have been a gruesome one. We knew it, and we were thankful beyond words that she had survived.

"Have you ever had a scare like that?" my dad asked Chocs.

"Not in all my years in Africa," he said.

"Do you ever carry a rifle?"

"In the past, we have not. At least, not in the Kalahari. But after today, I may change that policy."

Chocs went on to explain that the rhinos' aggressive behavior was due to their concern over the safety of their newborn babies. A baby rhino's eyesight is even worse than an adult's, so they couldn't see us well enough to know to stay away. The parents, however, knew that their babies might be in danger, and that's why they attacked.

Despite the scare, my mom somehow managed to keep her sense of humor.

"I know I'm the one who asked to stop," she said, "but next time we see a rhino, I vote we keep driving."

Everyone laughed, which helped calm our nerves just a little.

"I second that vote," said Jubjub.

"Agreed," Chocs said. "No more stopping for rhinos."

Chocs asked my mom if she wanted to return to camp for a rest, but she insisted we continue the day as planned. Chocs then jumped into the driver's seat and turned the ignition. Much to our surprise, the jeep started.

"I can't believe it still works after taking such a beating," my dad said.

"These jeeps are rhino proof," Chocs said with a smile.

I rested my head against the back of the seat and closed my eyes. We were safe. After such a terrible scare, that's a good feeling. But how long will it last? As the desert sun warmed my face, I considered just how much I had underestimated the risk you take when exploring the wilds of Africa. No matter how thorough your knowledge of animal behavior, you never really know what they're going to do. One predator might pay no attention to you. Another might tear you apart. As my mom later said, "A safari is safe ... until it isn't."

## GANNON

I thought for sure I'd be having nightmares about that crazy rhino rampage for the rest of my life. I literally couldn't stop my hands from shaking. I even sat on them to hide the fact that I was trembling from Wyatt, but the shakes traveled right up my arms and I started to think that maybe I'd suffered some sort of trauma and would need to get professional help to recover from this whole thing, but the moment we arrived at the Bushmen village all of my fear totally disappeared.

Dozens of children ran to the jeep as we drove up. They were cheering and clapping and when I climbed out of the vehicle the kids surrounded me and were tugging at my arms and wrapping themselves around my legs and laughing and shouting. One of the kids even jumped on my back and I gave him a piggyback ride into the village. I honestly felt like a celebrity being mobbed by a group of crazed fans.

Our new friends, the Naru Bushmen

In the village, the kids scattered, and we were greeted by the elders. They all nodded and bowed slightly and we all shook hands. This tribe has about eighty people, Chocs told us, and about thirty of them are children. One of the things that stood out to me was that some of the kids were basically wearing loincloths and nothing else even though it was still really cold outside. There was one small boy that was shivering and I knelt down beside him and hugged him to warm him up. He felt like an ice cube and his nose was running and he had this hacking cough and I really wanted to give him my jacket, but was afraid that giving it to one kid might be a problem when there were so many in the village who could use it. Still, I was about to take it off and put it over him when an elder woman noticed the boy shivering and came over. She wrapped him tightly in a blanket and wagged her finger at him and said a few words in the Bushmen language, which, if I had to guess, probably translated to something like: "Are you crazy wearing only that loincloth in this cold?"

A traditional Bushmen hut

Not all of the Bushmen were almost naked. Some were draped in homemade blankets with colorful patterns and still others wore random hand-me-downs that I guessed had been donated by previous visitors. One kid even had a New York Yankees baseball cap on his head. I wondered what this Bushmen child might think if he went to a baseball game in Yankee Stadium. It'd probably be so strange to him he'd think he had traveled to another planet.

An older man, his face creased with deep lines, gestured to us, sweeping his hand across the horizon—a welcome invitation, Chocs said, for us to tour the village.

The village had about ten mud huts and when I say mud I mean mud. To build a hut, Jubjub explained, branches and sticks are put into the ground and then mud is packed all around and when the mud hardens it's almost like concrete. A couple windows are cut out using sharp handmade tools and then more branches and sticks are propped on top for a roof. In the center of the village was a courtyard where women were making all kinds of crafts that they sell to visitors, like beaded jewelry and ornaments and stuff like that. A few hundred feet away from the living area was a small chicken coop with twenty or so chickens clucking around and a separate fenced area with a few scruffy-looking goats.

As we walked through the courtyard, the children surrounded us again and started singing and dancing. I got some video footage of their performance, but after a few minutes I put away the camera and joined the festivities. They were all having so much fun and every one of them had a big smile on their face, and I couldn't help myself, I just had to be part of it, so I danced into the circle and was humming along to their melody the best I could and stomping my feet in the dirt and snapping my fingers and doing the occasional spin move. The kids all slapped their knees and laughed hysterically as I put on a show. Wyatt eventually joined in too, and they laughed even harder at him, which is understandable, because he dances like some kind of rusty old robot that's in desperate need of a good oiling.

I really wished that I spoke the Bushmen's language so I could have conversations with everyone, but other than the Bushmen, I was told that not many people do. It's made up of sounds and clicks and it's all verbal, meaning there is no written version that you can study. Still, we were able to overcome the language barrier thanks to Chocs and Jubjub, who had spent enough time with the Bushmen to be able to translate some of their language into English. After we finished dancing and I had caught my breath, I asked Jubjub to translate a song the kids were singing so that I could write the lyrics in my journal, but she said this particular song didn't contain actual words, only sounds from a song ancestors had been singing since before a Bushmen language even existed. That totally blew my mind!

My mom was so taken by the children that she volunteered to lend a hand to the villagers who had just started building a new, bigger school hut so that more children could attend. The Bushmen way of life seemed so simple and carefree and the children were all so happy even though they had almost no possessions. Seeing how they were so content made me wonder why they even needed a school. Jubjub told me that the younger generation was encouraged to get an education so that they could learn to negotiate with the government to keep certain lands free from private ownership, otherwise they would continue to be run off by ranch owners and have no place to live.

"The Bushmen's traditional way of life is under threat," Jubjub said. "Sadly, it's a dying culture."

## WYATT
AUGUST 22, 4:35 PM
KALAHARI DESERT
20° CELSIUS, 68° FAHRENHEIT
SKIES CLEAR, WIND CALM

After we toured the Bushmen village, an elder woman led us into the desert with some of the children to show us how they gather food and water. We walked slowly, stepping cautiously over the dusty, dry land. I wasn't sure what the Bushmen were looking for, but I was keeping a sharp eye out for three things:

1) rhinos, for obvious reasons

2) spiders, which can be huge and poisonous in the Kalahari

3) black mambas, one of the most venomous snakes on earth

About a half hour into the trek, the elder woman bent over and picked up a brown twig about four inches long. She held it up and called to her children. They all gathered around and began digging in the spot where she had found the twig.

"When they find this particular twig," Jubjub explained, "they know that there is water underneath."

Searching for water in the Kalahari

How she spotted that twig, I have no idea. To me, it looked just like every other twig in the Kalahari, but she knew that because this twig was a slightly lighter shade than the others, it meant there was water below it. I watched as they dug, expecting them to uncover a natural spring. But after digging a two-foot hole, there was still no water in sight. Instead, they removed a round gourd the size of a basketball. They then took a long stick and began rubbing it over the gourd's surface, creating a pulp that they piled up in the dirt. Once they had a handful of pulp, they packed it into a ball, held it over their mouths and squeezed. Sure enough, water dripped from the pulp. Each handful of pulp produced about an ounce of water.

It amazed me, the work that went into getting a single sip of water. I felt guilty about having two liters of bottled water in my backpack. Watching the Bushmen drink from the shaved gourd, it made me sick to think of how much water most of us waste every day. We take long showers, leave the faucet running, and dump out the rest of a glass of water when we're no longer thirsty. Truth is, we take water for granted. I swore to myself then and there that I'd never again waste another drop.

## GANNON
LATE AFTERNOON

Sitting here against the trunk of this thorny bush, looking out at this stark desert landscape of rocks and sand and bony shrubs, watching the Bushmen share a potato they just dug out of the dirt, the concept of a restaurant or grocery store where food and drinks are available in such abundance is almost hard to imagine. Thank heavens they exist, though, because trekking through the bush this afternoon something has become very obvious—if I had to survive in the Kalahari, alone, I'd be buzzard meat in no time flat. No ifs, ands, or buts. Even if I were taught how to find those tiny twigs in the sand and dig up a gourd, I'd still be in trouble. I mean, you'd have to find ten a day just to squeeze out a couple glasses' worth of water. And let's be honest here, it's not really water. Calling it water is like calling asparagus a candy cane. It'd be more accurate to call it "a milky-type, pulpy liquid that's really bitter" or, if that's too long, "gourd juice" would probably get the point across just as well. Sampling a few drops, I had to turn away to hide the fact that I was gagging. The Bushmen are able to exist on very little water, so a few sips a day is really all they need to survive, but that wouldn't work so well for me.

Along with the gourd and potatoes, the Bushmen collected a bag full of sticks that they use to clean their teeth. One of the boys gave me a demonstration, scrubbing his teeth with the stick just like you would with a toothbrush. These sticks must work pretty well because most of the Bushmen have great teeth and I think it's safe to say that there aren't any dentists out here in the Kalahari.

The elder woman is satisfied with all that we've found and has plopped down in the sand to smoke a cigarette. Out of respect, we are all sitting around and waiting patiently until she is finished. The tobacco, Chocs said, was a gift from previous visitors. I could think of a much better gift for the Bushmen than cigarettes, but I'm going to keep my mouth shut.

## WYATT

AUGUST 23, 5:53 AM
KALAHARI DESERT, EDO'S CAMP
4° CELSIUS, 40° FAHRENHEIT
SKIES CLEAR, WIND 5-10 MPH

It's not even light yet, but my dad is already up and preparing for a day photographing the white rhinos. In spite of our frightening encounter yesterday, he can't wait to get up close and personal with the beasts. He's also set up an easel near the watering hole, so that he can make a painting when the rhinos come to drink in the evening.

My mom, obviously wanting nothing to do with rhinos, is going to go back to the Bushmen village to begin building the school hut.

I am going to join Chocs and my dad on their rhino expedition. Gannon is going back to the Bushmen village with Jubjub and mom. It was tough for me to decide what I wanted to do today. Both are unique adventures, not to mention tremendous learning experiences, so I decided to divide my time down the middle. Today I'll go in search of the rhinos; tomorrow I'll go to the Bushmen village.

# GANNON

When I got to the dining tent this morning for breakfast, I had the pleasure of meeting Tcori (Te-cor-ee), another member of the Bushmen tribe who had just returned from an expedition in the Okavango Delta.

Tcori is the son of the elder I met the day before. Like his father he is skinny and short, probably no more than five feet tall, if I had to guess. Also like his father, Tcori's face is weathered and marked with lines from years of exposure to the harsh African sun. It would be pretty difficult to guess how old he is, because his body is lean and muscular and could easily pass for the body of a teenager, but his face, with all the lines, looks a lot older. When I asked, Jubjub explained that Tcori didn't know his age because the Bushmen don't follow any sort of calendar so they have no way of knowing how old they are. Bushmen, I guess, have no use for such information. I kind of like that. No calendar, no birthday, no age. It made me think, what's it really matter anyway?

Tcori wears a tan cloth wrapped around his waist and a beaded necklace and like the other Bushmen, his feet are small, coarse, and bare. I can't imagine walking around the Kalahari without shoes. I mean, it seems totally insane to me. The bottoms of my feet would be torn to shreds before I'd taken ten steps, but after I watched Tcori walk over thorn bushes, jagged rocks, and hot sand without even seeming to notice, I realized that a pair of shoes would be of no use to him. A lifetime of walking through the desert has made the soles of his feet as tough as leather. I'd be willing to bet Wyatt's beloved microscope that Tcori could walk over hot coals without even flinching.

The most fascinating thing about Tcori isn't that he walks around barefoot. It's that he carries a spear. I kid you not. An honest-to-goodness spear. The neck of the spear is made from a Marula branch that has been shaved smooth and the arrow is carved out of elephant bone. As I looked at it, all jagged and sharp and stained with blood, I couldn't help but wonder just how many times he'd used it to bring home food to his people in the village. We were told that Tcori was one of the last remaining hunters in his tribe.

After Tcori had been introduced to everyone, we learned that he had come to us with a message. While in the delta, he got wind that a poacher had shot and wounded a female lion and to make matters worse, the lioness had four young cubs! The lions were able to escape from the poacher, but he was tracking them and would definitely finish the job if someone didn't stop him.

Hearing this news just about sent me off the deep end. I literally couldn't stop pacing around and running my hands through my hair like a nervous lunatic. I mean, how could someone do something like that? There was no question in my mind: it was up to us to save the lions!

"If we don't help them, who will?" I yelled. "You heard Tcori! The poacher will catch the lioness and her cubs before long, and when he does he'll kill them! Come on, we have to do something!"

If Chocs hadn't settled me down, I would have probably jumped in a truck and sped off to the airstrip by myself. I tend to react passionately when something is really important to me. Some people might even say I overreact. Maybe I do. Whatever. That's just the way I'm wired, I guess. Anyway, the rest of our group was more levelheaded. We all sat down in the dining tent and discussed our options. Right now, Chocs is trying to reach a local pilot on the radio to see if he is available to fly us to the Okavango Delta.

## WYATT

AUGUST 23, 9:14 AM
KALAHARI DESERT, EDO'S CAMP
16° CELSIUS, 60° FAHRENHEIT
SKIES CLEARING, WIND 5-10 MPH

Typically, humans shouldn't interact with wild animals under any circumstances. It's an unwritten law. In the wilderness, we must allow nature to take its course. But this is different. The lioness was shot by a poacher. And being shot illegally, with a high-powered rifle, is not an act of nature in my book. If the lioness had been injured in some other way, say, for example, she had broken her leg and was dying because she could not hunt for food, we would not get involved. That may seem cruel, but again, it's the law of nature, and we've learned that in Africa no animal ever dies in vain. They feed off one another. When one animal dies, it helps another animal survive. It's the circle of life in action.

The lioness will not live long with a gunshot wound. This puts her cubs at great risk. For the first year of their lives, lion cubs feed on their mother's milk, and these cubs are only a few weeks old. If the mother dies, so will the cubs. Even if they are able to escape the poacher, they will face the danger of another predator. Most people think lions aren't challenged in the wild. But lions actually have an enemy who is strong enough to attack and kill them. That enemy is the hyena, and there are thousands of them on the delta.

"Some experts estimate there to be fewer than 30,000 lions left in the wild today," Chocs told us. "Their numbers have decreased significantly since the early 1990s, when it was believed the lion population was over 100,000."

Learning this only confirmed what I already knew. We had to help these lions!

Chocs, Jubjub and Tcori are loading up a jeep with a week's worth of supplies: food, water, tents, sleeping bags and a medical kit. I also saw Chocs packing a rifle, which makes me a little nervous. I suppose it's better to have a rifle and not need it, than to need one and not have it. I'm always up for adventure, but our safari has turned into something much more serious.

My parents gave the thumbs-up for Gannon and me to

go along, provided Chocs promised to keep us at a safe distance from the wildlife.

"I assure you," Chocs said to my parents, "we will take every precaution. Tcori knows the bush better than anyone. If we searched the continent over, we could not find a better guide. Should you allow your sons to join us, it will be a tremendous learning experience for them."

I think it was this last part about it being a learning experience that ultimately sold my parents.

Jubjub is going, too. However, she will stay at the main camp and act as our radio contact while we search for the lioness. The radio antenna at camp sends a signal as far as Maun, so Jubjub will be able to contact the authorities if we run into trouble.

I need to finish up this journal entry and check to make sure that I've packed all the necessary supplies. In less than an hour, we will make our way to the airstrip, where a pilot will be waiting to fly us to the Okavango Delta. From there, we will embark on our mission. I can't ignore the fact that we are venturing into a hostile environment. There will be predators, snakes, disease-carrying insects, and venomous spiders, any of which could bring our expedition to a disastrous end. I am confident, however, that with Tcori's guidance we will be safe and our mission to save the lioness and her cubs will be successful.

# PART II

## SEARCH FOR THE LIONESS AND HER CUBS

Flying over the Okavango Delta

# GANNON

We've just passed over the western edge of the delta. The colors of the landscape below us have changed from browns and reds to blues and greens. Such an amazing contrast with the Kalahari being so barren and full of sand and rock and scraggly bushes and the delta being so lush with all kinds of rivers and lakes and giant trees. I'd love to write more, but our plane is getting tossed all over the place by some strong winds, and I've already explained how that makes me feel.

Signing off until later . . .

# WYATT

AUGUST 23, 8:23 PM
OKAVANGO DELTA, 19° 07′ S 23° 09′ E
18° CELSIUS, 64° FAHRENHEIT
ELEVATION: 3,021 FEET
SKIES HAZY, WIND CALM

Shinde Camp will be our headquarters while we're in the delta. A small camp hidden in a forest, Shinde has a dozen or so large tents, including a dining tent and a deck with a fire pit.

We arrived too late in the day to search for the lioness, so we decided to stay overnight at Shinde and go out at first light. Once we have picked up the trail of the lioness, we'll set up camps in the bush each night until we find her.

As it got dark, we sat around a fire and listened as the nocturnal animals came to life all around us. Singing birds, howling baboons, laughing hippos, and trumpeting elephants were all within earshot of camp. One thing is very clear: We're on the animals' turf now.

Chocs explained the differences between the Okavango Delta and the Kalahari.

"In the Okavango, wildlife is much more abundant than it is in the Kalahari," Chocs said. "Lions, hippos, elephants, leopards, and Cape buffalo can wander through camp at any time. These animals are very active at night. So after dinner you will be escorted to your tent. Once you are inside, do not leave under any circumstances. If you venture out, you will be in danger. You may even hear animals walking past your tent during the night. Just keep quiet. They'll usually move along."

"Usually?" I said. "Well, what if they don't?"

"Don't worry," Chocs said with a laugh, "they almost always do."

Nothing against Chocs, but after the rhino attack, I find it hard to trust him completely. I know he means well and is confident that we aren't in any danger as long as we do what we're told, but if the experience in the Kalahari taught us anything, it's that your safety is never guaranteed in the African bush.

## GANNON

EARLY MORNING, STILL INSIDE THE TENT

Picture this: total darkness! So dark that you can't even see your hand two inches from your face! My brother and I are on cots inside a small tent. Mosquito nets are draped over the cots to protect us from bugs, and we have a thick down blanket to keep us warm. It's so quiet I can practically hear my heart beat—thump-thump . . . thump-thump . . . thump-thump. The only other sound is the soft buzz of the insects, awake and singing under the delta moonlight.

Then, in the not-so-far-off distance, I hear what sounds like a roar. Of course, this makes my heartbeat quicken and I get even more nervous when I touch the canvas walls of the tent and suddenly realize that they'll do very little to stop a hungry predator from getting to us.

The darkness becomes too much to handle, so I unclip my flashlight from my backpack and shine it in Wyatt's face.

"Wyatt," I whisper, "you awake?"

"Yes," he says, without opening his eyes.

"Did you hear that?"

"I did."

"What was it?"

"I don't know."

"Do you think it was a lion?"

"Probably."

"What do you mean, probably? What other animals roar like that?"

"None that I know of."

"So you think it was definitely a lion?"

"Yes. It was a lion, okay. Go to sleep."

"How am I supposed to sleep when I know there is a lion walking around outside our tent?"

Just then, I hear another roar, and then another.

"Oh, man. There's more than one lion, and it sounds like they're coming this way."

"I bet they're tracking your scent. Probably think you're a buffalo."

"I showered today. You're the one that stinks."

"Go to sleep."

"Are you kidding? I'm not going to sleep a wink."

"Then why don't you go out there and shoo them away?"

"Very funny."

Inside each tent is a blow horn. These horns are left in the tents for emergencies. If you have an emergency you are supposed to blow the horn and at the sound of the horn an armed guard will come running to your rescue ... or so we've been told.

Assuming that lions entering our tent to tear us limb from limb would be considered an emergency, I take the blow horn off the nightstand. With the horn in hand, I feel more prepared to fend off an attack, but then a thought crosses my mind. What if the horn doesn't work? What if I press the button and nothing happens? What if there is a manufacturing defect? What if this horn is a stinking dud? I curse myself for not testing it before we all settled into our tents for the night and think long and hard about blowing it for safe measure. "Why not?" I reason. "Better safe than sorry." Then again, if I blow the horn and the guard jumps out of his bed and comes running through the bush in his underpants only to find that there is not, in fact, an honest-to-goodness emergency, Chocs may begin to doubt that Wyatt and I are worthy of joining him on this expedition.

"Why did I bring these kids with me, anyway?" he might ask himself. "The Okavango Delta is no place for immature boys."

I don't want him to have that sort of impression of us. My brother and I have been in many frightening situations before, and given these experiences, I'm pretty sure our courage would measure up to that of the bravest teenager, but this is our first encounter with the king of the beasts, so I'm really nervous and have absolutely no clue what to expect.

Okay, the roars have trailed off, which makes me think the lions are moving away from camp. Maybe they decided to go after an animal with a little more meat on its bones, which is smart on the lions' part. Together, Wyatt and I would hardly qualify as an appetizer for a hungry lion. Still, just to make myself feel more comfortable, I'm keeping the blow horn close, in my hand actually, with my finger on the button, ready to sound that sucker at a moment's notice.

A male lion rests before the evening prowl

# WYATT

I'm sitting outside our tent, writing in my journal by the flickering light of a kerosene lantern. The sun hasn't come up yet, and it's cold. I am wrapped in a wool blanket and drinking hot chocolate that I made on our small camp stove. The benefit of colder weather is that there are fewer bugs. The Centers for Disease Control and Prevention has the Okavango Delta listed as an official malaria area. I am taking malaria medication as a precaution, though I haven't seen a single mosquito since I got here. I have seen a spider, unfortunately. It was hanging out near my tent. The thing was a beast, too, probably big enough to eat a mouse. With the help of a very long stick, I chased it away.

I can hear some kind of animal moving through the bushes not far from where I sit. It is still too dark to make out what it is, but I do know this: It's BIG! I'm staying very still in the hopes that I will not attract this animal's attention.

I slept decently last night, but it sure is eerie to hear so many animals outside your tent. You lie there thinking to yourself, "What in the world is that? It sure sounds like something big, and if it's big, then that means it's also dangerous. Darn it, I just remembered that I left a candy bar in my backpack. How could I be so stupid? I hope the animal doesn't smell it and claw its way in for a snack."

But, despite such nagging fears, we survived the night, and I was able to sleep four or five hours. I don't think Gannon slept at all.

Today we will set off into the delta in search of the lioness. I have to admit, my nerves are beginning to get the better of me. I hope we get to the lioness in time and don't run into the poacher along the way. In these situations, it is always the waiting part that kills me. The sooner we leave, the better.

The sun is beginning to illuminate the delta wilderness. I can see just enough to make out the animal in the bushes nearby. It's a giant bull elephant . . . and I mean GIANT! His tusks have to weigh 100 pounds each! I'm remaining as still as possible, my only movement being my hand scribbling in my journal. It's one thing to see an elephant at the zoo, but to see an elephant grazing right next to your tent, that's a completely different experience altogether.

An elephant eating outside our tent

# GANNON

A little after the sun came up we piled all of our supplies into the safari jeep and said good-bye to Jubjub and the Shinde staff and set off into the delta. I was really hungry and hoping for a big, hot breakfast, but we were in such a hurry that there wasn't time for us to sit down to a full meal, so Jubjub packed us each a bag of biscuits and some dried fruits to take along. As Chocs said, "Every minute counts." It was cold early on but the sun is out and it's warmed up nicely. We've been driving now for a few hours, at least, so we decided to take a short break from the bumpy ride and have a snack.

Out here in the bush there is just nature and nothing else. The feeling of being so far away from everything is really kind of mind-blowing. We're totally disconnected out here. There are no cell phones. No TVs or computers. I will not be watching the news or writing email or texting or going online. While I'm out here, I will have no idea what is going on in the rest of the world and there is something really nice about that.

At first, being in such a remote place felt kind of strange. I mean, without a cell phone, TV, or computer, it seemed like I'd have nothing to do, so I thought for sure that I'd get bored stiff in no time. I've become used to having all these things to occupy my time, but when you think about it, they're really nothing more than distractions that take you out of the present. What I'm trying to say, I guess, is that these days no one seems to live in the moment. It's almost like we're losing sight of things that are right in front of our face.

Our Okavango safari jeep

My brother would probably quote Charles Darwin and say that we have "evolved" and that these distractions have become part of who we are. But out here, the rat race that goes on in other parts of the world is totally insignificant. In lots of ways, life is simplified in the bush. All I really need is something to eat, something to drink, and a place to sleep. And that's it, which leaves me with lots of time to think and to notice the things that I typically overlook when I'm at home. Out here, you are forced to notice the food you eat, for example, to look at it and really taste it, instead of shoveling it down while you try to do five other things. You are forced to listen to a person speak until they have finished their thought, instead of interrupting them to answer a phone or read a text or check your email. You are forced to live in the moment, because that's all there is. For me, it's kind of like my senses have awakened from some long coma and my brain has gotten rid of all the clutter that was bogging it down. Everything seems clear.

Okay, enough with the philosophical mumbo jumbo. Chocs just told us that it's time to get moving.

On with the adventure . . .

## WYATT

AUGUST 24, 10:47 PM
OKAVANGO DELTA
14° CELSIUS, 58° FAHRENHEIT
SKIES CLEAR, WIND 5-10 MPH

I can't believe how much wildlife there is in the Okavango Delta! We've passed elephants, zebras, wildebeests, giraffes, warthogs, impala, hippos, and Cape buffalos, all by the dozens! Scientists estimate that there are as many as 260,000 large mammals and 500 bird species in the Okavango Delta, and I don't doubt it for a second. I was so overwhelmed by the incredible number of animals we saw today, I almost forgot about the poor lioness.

But every now and then Chocs would stop the jeep and Tcori would step out and quietly move through the bush to look at something in the grass or pick up something from the ground or check the markings on a tree. Tcori learned to track animals from his grandparents in the Kalahari. Watching him work was a reminder that we aren't on a typical safari.

Just before sundown, Tcori tore several branches and leaves from a bush and put them in his satchel.

"Inside that bush is a sticky sap that can be smeared on an arrowhead and used as poison," Chocs explained.

"But why does Tcori need poison?" Gannon asked. "We're not going to kill any animals, are we?"

"A small dose of the poison will not kill a large animal," Chocs explained, "but it is powerful enough to knock the animal unconscious. Tcori will use this poison on the lioness so that she will sleep while we remove the bullet."

I'd never thought about how we would remove the bullet from the lioness, but I suppose she wouldn't just let us walk right up and start poking around her wound. Keeping her unconscious is not only the safe thing to do, it's the humane thing to do.

Shortly before dark, we set up an overnight camp—four tents in some flat grass near a narrow waterway. The type of tent we are using has two tarps, each hanging over a wooden frame in the shape of an upside down V. The larger tarp goes on top, providing shade and protecting us from bad weather.

The smaller tarp hangs underneath the larger tarp, allowing just enough space for one person to sleep.

After putting up the tents, we had a simple dinner of rice and beans, and a cup of hot tea. There is something about camping that makes any food taste good, no matter how boring the meal. Maybe it has something to do with the process of preparing a meal over a fire while you sit out under the stars. I do love the process and when all was said and done tonight's simple, yet hot meal sure did taste good.

A family of hippos feeds along the riverbank

After dinner, everyone else settled into their tents. But I stayed up, sitting alone by the campfire, enjoying the incredible night sky. The fact that Chocs had a rifle in his tent lessened my fears somewhat, but to tell the truth, I was still a bit jumpy. When a warthog sprang from the nearby bushes, I was so startled I fell over and scrambled to my tent faster than you can say "goodnight."

## GANNON

AUGUST 25
3:21 AM

For the second straight night, I can't sleep! I'm inside my tent, tucked comfortably into my sleeping bag and my mind is buzzing with all these crazy thoughts despite trying just about everything I know to slow it down, even counting sheep. Nothing has worked. Every time I close my eyes I see those crazy, black vulture eyes staring at me—all beady and demon-like and just locked on me, almost like they're marking me for death.

Let me explain.

After lunch we continued driving through the delta over the lumpy terrain, bouncing around in our seats as we passed just about every animal imaginable. The sun was out and the wind was a little cool, but just warm enough and I felt really good with almost no fear. I mean, what was there to worry about? We were safe. But sometime later in the afternoon, we stopped so that Tcori could poke around and find some flat, dry land for our camp. He hopped out of the jeep and was strolling around casually, just looking here and there and checking out the location when suddenly he stopped dead in his tracks. I thought he must have seen a pride of lions nearby, but then I noticed there was something above us that had caught his eye. Naturally, I looked up to see what it was. Perched on a high tree branch was a vulture.

I mean, there's really no nice way to say it, so I'll just come out and be honest—vultures are hideous creatures. And the way it just stared and stared and wouldn't turn away, jeez, I couldn't help but think it was a bad sign. A real bad one!

After spotting the vulture, Tcori told Chocs that we had to find another location to camp for the night. Something about that ugly vulture had bothered Tcori, that's for sure, and if something bothers Tcori, it bothers me.

Before we left, I took out my video camera and filmed the nasty old bird, trying my best to get a nice, steady close-up. I was happy with the footage, but as we drove on, the terrifying gaze of that repulsive scavenger kept appearing in my mind. And here's the worst part, when I looked up in the sky again, some ways down the line from where we had stopped, there it was, circling high overhead. I couldn't believe it. Was it actually following us? And if so, why? That's what I wanted to know. Did it think we were goners? Four more casualties of the African bush? Is that it? Did that ugly bird think we were going to be its next meal?

Oh, man, that thing has got me all freaked out. It's coming up on 4:00 a.m. now and we have a long day ahead of us and I need rest but I'm still awake and restless and very afraid of what dangers might lie in our path.

That old, nasty buzzard

# WYATT

AUGUST 25, 9:32 AM
OKAVANGO DELTA, 19° 10' S 22° 51' E
16° CELSIUS, 62° FAHRENHEIT
SKIES HAZY, WIND CALM

Early this morning, disaster struck. Not far from camp we drove up to a waterway that was probably 300 feet wide from shore to shore. Chocs said he'd driven through this stretch of water many times in the past and was sure the vehicle would have no problem reaching the other side.

"These safari jeeps are built for this sort of travel," he said. "The engine is sealed off, and the snorkel extends four feet higher so that the engine can draw enough air to operate even when it's completely underwater."

Chocs confidently drove the jeep into the water without a second thought. The first thirty yards or so were smooth going. It reminded me of being in a boat. A low wake trailed behind us. Then the water got deeper, and it began to pour over the side, filling the interior. I lifted my feet onto the seat to keep my shoes from getting drenched. As the water got deeper, the jeep started to look like a submarine trolling on the surface of the ocean. The seats, roll bars, and hood were the only parts of the jeep above the water line. But the engine trudged on.

"When I'm old enough to drive, I want a jeep just like this one," Gannon said.

"Me too," I said. "Think of the adventures we could go on in the Rocky Mountains."

As Gannon and I dreamed of one day having our own safari jeeps, our vehicle was jolted and came to a stop. Chocs jumped up on the seat and looked around.

"Uh-oh," he said.

"Uh-oh?" I repeated. "That doesn't sound good."

"We've hit something," he said.

"A hippo?" Gannon asked.

"If it were a hippo, it would have flipped the jeep by now. It's probably just a rock."

Chocs backed up and tried to go around whatever was blocking our path. Again the vehicle came to a sudden stop. The water was crystal clear, so he stood up and looked over the hood, but the underwater algae and grasses made it impossible to see what we'd hit.

"I'm going in for a closer look," Chocs said and waded into the water. He moved to the front of the vehicle and sank underneath. After a good thirty seconds, he came back up, wiping water from his face.

"There's a tree trunk under the water," he said. "It's too big to go over it, so we'll have to go downstream and see if we can drive around it."

But when we backed up, the wheels lost their traction and started to spin. Chocs tried everything he could, but the jeep wasn't going anywhere. Then to make matters worse, the engine died. Chocs tried several times to restart it, but it was no use.

"Grab your things," Chocs said. "It looks like we're going to have to swim for it."

I had a slight problem with this plan, but it had nothing to do with the swimming part. I can swim. The problem was the giant crocodile sleeping on the shore. Without question, this was the biggest croc I'd ever seen. I kid you not. It had to be fifteen feet long! Chocs said that if we kept quiet and didn't splash around too much, the croc probably wouldn't wake up.

"He probably won't wake up?" I said. "Well for sake of argument, let's just say that he does? Then what?"

"If the croc wakes up," Chocs said with a smile, "just swim faster."

His answer didn't comfort me in the least. Even if the sleeping croc didn't wake up, who's to say that one of his buddies wasn't hiding just under the water's surface some-where nearby? Then again, we were stuck dead smack in the middle of the waterway. What other choice did we have but to swim?

"We're heading straight for that beach," Chocs said as he pointed to a beach approximately 150 feet from where we sat in the stalled jeep. "That way, we'll be swimming with the current."

We gathered our supplies and loaded them into three waterproof duffels. With our supplies sealed off, we waded into the water. Where we stood, it was nearly chest deep. I began moving quietly through the water in the direction of the slow current, slipping along the muddy bottom toward shore.

I hadn't been in the water thirty seconds when something slammed into my shoulder. My worst fear was suddenly realized. A croc was attacking!

I screamed for help and spun around to fight for my life. Behind me I saw the long, spiny back of a giant croc floating just above the water's surface. I swung my fist down on top of it again and again, screaming all the while.

Somehow in the middle of my panic, I remembered having read about a guy who survived an attack by poking the croc in the eyes. As I searched frantically for an eye to gouge, I realized that the creature I was battling wasn't actually a croc at all. In fact, it wasn't even a creature. It was, much to my relief, a log. That's right. A big, slimy log!

My relief quickly turned into humiliation. I felt so foolish for fighting a harmless piece of bark. Even worse, Gannon saw the whole thing. He was laughing so hard he could barely breathe. And I know from past experiences that he'll never let me hear the end of it. I'm not kidding. We'll be ninety years old, relaxing on the front porch in our favorite rocking chairs, and he'll say, "Hey, Wyatt. You remember that time in Botswana when you were so savagely attacked by that log?"

But there was no time to stew over my brother's amusement. I hadn't even caught my breath when I heard Chocs yell.

"The croc's awake! Swim for it, boys!"

I turned just in time to see the giant croc waddling into the water. All of my yelling and splashing woke him up, and he didn't seem too happy about it. We all swam as fast as we could toward the shore, but the croc was closing in on us fast, its tail slithering like a snake in the calm water. When you're being chased by a croc, it feels like you're moving in super slow motion, regardless of how fast you're actually swimming. Luckily, we were swimming just fast enough. When we finally climbed ashore the croc was still a good fifty feet behind us.

Floating on top of the water, he stared at us as if to say, "You got lucky this time, but I wouldn't try it again if I were you."

Don't worry, Mr. Croc. We won't.

One of the many giant crocs that calls the Okavango home

# GANNON

Okay, Wyatt's a pro when it comes to embarrassing himself, but that whole mistaking-a-log-for-a-croc incident might just top every moronic thing he's ever done in his life. After rolling around on shore laughing until my stomach hurt, it dawned on me: We had a very serious situation on our hands. Our transportation was stuck in the middle of a waterway and there was no way to get it out!

Chocs radioed Jubjub at camp.

"Chocs to Shinde Camp. Come in, Shinde."

"Jubjub here. How is everything going?"

"Not so good. The jeep is stuck in deep water. We need someone to drive the other jeep to us so we can pull it out."

"Well," Jubjub said, "I'm afraid that's not possible."

Turns out, the other jeep is out of commission, too. A mechanic is working on the engine, but Jubjub says it needs several new parts that will have to be flown in from Maun. At best, the jeep will be fixed in four days.

I mean, what kind of luck is that? Seriously? I knew that vulture was a bad sign.

"Okay, Jubjub," Chocs said. "I suppose there's nothing more you can do. Keep us posted on the progress of the vehicle. I'll radio you again later."

"Okay, Dad. Be safe out there."

"I will. I love you."

"Love you, too. Over and out."

Chocs set down the radio and turned to us.

"Gentlemen," he said very matter-of-factly. "It looks like we're on our own. From here on out, we'll travel by foot."

Fine, whatever, at this stage of the game we really have no choice, but here's the problem: Being on foot increases the level of danger a thousandfold. Before setting out from Shinde, Chocs told us that when we're in the truck the animals see the vehicle and all of its passengers as one very large animal—a large animal that they don't want to mess with—so they are unlikely to attack. Now, this made total sense to me and would have been completely believable, that is, if we hadn't already had an experience that completely contradicted what he was saying.

"Uh, Chocs," I said. "What about the rhinos that attacked our jeep?"

"Oh," Chocs said, almost as if he had already forgotten, "well, that was the exception."

On foot we're just four weak little human beings walking around like a bunch of juicy drumsticks. That's not to say a predator will attack on sight and scarf us down if it happens to be hungry. Even though we don't match the strength of these predators, they view humans as a threat and usually try their best to avoid confrontation. Again, as Chocs said, there are exceptions to the rule and those exceptions are what worry me.

We're heading out soon. To prep us for our journey, Chocs just translated some important bush wisdom from Tcori.

"If we encounter a lion," he said, "do not run. Even if the lion charges, do not run. It is most likely a mock charge, meaning the lion is only trying to size you up and see if you are really a threat. In this case, a lion will halt his charge and turn away. But if you run, the lion will chase you, and if that happens you're in trouble. What you need to do is keep eye contact with the lion and back away slowly. If you try to hide behind a tree or lie down, a lion might become curious and move in for a closer look, and if that happens you're in trouble as well."

"Just to make sure I understand this correctly," I said, "the idea is to stay out of trouble."

"Precisely," Chocs said with a toothy grin.

Okay, just for the record, if we do happen upon a lion and it does decide to charge, I'm not so sure I'll be able to hold my ground. If I'm not mistaken, there's something called the "fight or flight" response that is embedded in our brains at birth. If a lion were bearing down on me, I know one thing: My brain would choose "flight." I mean, isn't it human nature to run from something that can tear you limb from limb?

Oh, man, I just hope that I'm able to remember this advice and not freak out like Wyatt did when he encountered the tree-stump croc. To improve my chances of reacting like we're supposed to, I made up a little saying that I'm repeating quietly to myself. It goes like this: "Stay calm, keep eye contact, and back away slowly . . . Repeat." My hope is that if I say it enough it will become ingrained in my mind and I'll be able to overcome the "fight or flight" thing and react appropriately.

All these dangers aside, the aspiring filmmaker in me can't help but see this adventure as a chance to get some amazing footage. I honestly can't think of anything more intense than capturing a charging lion on film—his mane drawn back in the wind, a dust cloud swirling behind it, his eyes locked on the camera. That kind of footage would put me in the ranks of some of the great wildlife filmmakers of all time—that is, if I could keep my hands from shaking so bad that people would think I'd filmed an earthquake.

Knowing that Chocs has a rifle and that he and Tcori have a lifetime of experience in the bush makes me feel a little better about our chances of surviving this journey. Both of them know how to navigate the African wilderness, and more importantly, how to behave around animals. Without them, Wyatt and I would definitely slip a few notches on the food chain.

Chocs and Tcori seem to think that abandoning the jeep was probably a blessing in disguise because the lioness was shot by a poacher driving a truck and would probably run at the first sound of an approaching vehicle. According to Tcori, on foot we'll have a much better chance of finding the lioness and her cubs.

In a few minutes we'll continue moving south until an

hour or so before it gets dark. That's when we'll scout out a good location to set up camp and stay the night. Fingers crossed all goes well.

## WYATT
AUGUST 25, 11:47 PM
OKAVANGO DELTA
13° CELSIUS, 55° FAHRENHEIT
SKIES CLEAR, WIND CALM

I am awake and, to be completely honest, not feeling as strong as I would like. I think the day's excitement, combined with the long trek through the bush, has sapped me of all my energy. It is difficult even to write, but I have to make a few notes about our experience with the elephants today.

Walking along a dried-out riverbed, we encountered for the first time the sad consequences of poaching. Under the shade of the trees, we saw a female elephant lying on her side with a severe wound to her right hind leg. She had stepped into a poacher's trap, and a wire snare was wrapped tightly around the lower part of her leg. The snare had torn through the elephant's tough skin, and the wound had become terribly infected. The infection was so bad the elephant could no longer walk.

Tcori said there was nothing we could do. This poor elephant was dying, and it was only a matter of time before the scavengers moved in to feast on her remains. Once the scavengers had done their job, the poacher would return to collect the tusks. In an effort to prevent this, Chocs radioed the elephant's coordinates to Jubjub, who, in turn, radioed the authorities. It is the practice of the government to remove a dead elephant's tusks and store them in a vault. They do this to keep the tusks out of the poachers' hands.

A large bull elephant circled the female elephant like a husband mourning his wife. With his tusks, the bull tried desperately to lift his companion. It was as if the bull would not accept the sad fate of his mate. It even appeared that the bull was crying. Chocs explained that elephants have glands located just behind their eyes that excrete a fluid when they get stressed. This fluid, which streams down the side of an elephant's face, looks like tears.

To me, the tears were proof that the bull elephant was sad. People think animals don't feel. That's not true; animals do feel and some, like the elephant, show great emotion.

With that, I must now close this entry. I am feeling weaker and more feverish with each passing minute. I have to get some rest if I hope to feel better by morning.

## GANNON
AUGUST 26
2:07 PM


It's official. There's no disputing it. Just as I thought, the vulture was a bad omen. Our expedition is cursed!

First, there was the jeep, then we come across the dying

elephant—which, for the record, was one of the most awful things I've ever witnessed and made me so upset that I can't even write about it—and now, to top it all off, Wyatt's sick.

He woke up this morning with a high fever and the chills and he was all pale and looked terrible. Before the trip, my mom told us about the different illnesses people can get in Africa. Of course, we took steps to protect ourselves from lots of them. Like, for example, we're taking malaria medication, so we highly doubt that Wyatt has malaria. And we were also vaccinated for hepatitis A and B, polio, typhoid, and yellow fever, but there are lots of other illnesses that have no vaccination. Dengue fever, which you can get from mosquitoes, is one example of a nasty illness you really can't do anything to protect yourself from, well, other than wearing bug repellent, but the thing is, we haven't seen many mosquitoes since we got here because of the cool temperatures and all. Wyatt does have a few small welts from some kind of bug bite. I remember reading that tsetse flies could be found throughout sub-Saharan Africa and that a bite from one of these bumblebee-sized insects could cause "African sleeping sickness," which is pretty serious and causes fatigue, aching muscles and joints, and really bad headaches. So I thought maybe that's what is making him sick, because he has all those symptoms, but Chocs told me that tsetse flies were eradicated from Botswana years ago.

Other than insects, I'm told there are all kinds of bacteria in the delta water that can definitely mess with your system.

This bacteria doesn't bother the natives. They've grown up drinking the water, so I guess their digestive systems are used to it, but the bacteria are foreign to us and can cause all kinds of intestinal problems if swallowed. We've been boiling most of our drinking water and that kills the bacteria and other bad stuff and we also have a small supply of iodine tablets to purify the water when we don't have time to boil it. Wyatt and I haven't had a drop of untreated water that I know of, unless he swallowed some when we swam ashore. Maybe that's it, who knows?

With Wyatt being too weak to travel and all, our search for the lioness has been put on hold. Tcori spent a lot of time in the bush today, gathering roots and things that the Bushmen use to treat fever. While he was out he found signs of the lioness and her cubs and thinks that we'll reach them soon. I know the clock is ticking and I want to get to the lioness right away, but the most important thing is Wyatt's health.

Right now, Tcori is boiling up the roots to make some kind of concoction for Wyatt. I've got my fingers crossed that this Bushmen brew works some real magic. If his condition gets much worse we'll have to abandon our search completely and if that happens the lioness and her cubs will definitely die and I don't even want to think about that. Seeing that poor elephant today and with Wyatt sick and all, I'm just in an unhappy sort of mood and the thought of the lions dying makes it even worse.

Another thing that's bothering me is that I haven't sent a message to our parents about Wyatt. I actually told Jubjub not to. Not yet, at least. I mean, there's nothing they can do so I don't want to worry them if this all turns out to be nothing. There's not a whole lot we can do, either, and that's the frustrating part. There are no doctors in the bush, so when you get sick out here, you're on your own. I have faith in the Bushmen remedies, but if the situation gets bad enough, Jubjub can ask the authorities in Maun to call for an airlift to the capital city of Gaborone, where there is a hospital. I really hope it doesn't come to this. If it does, it'll mean Wyatt's life is in danger.

## GANNON

AUGUST 27
MIDDLE OF THE NIGHT

I'm in Wyatt's tent so that I can monitor him during the night. I wish I could report some good news, but unfortunately things are getting worse. It doesn't seem like Tcori's remedies did much for him, if anything at all. His temperature has been between 103 and 105 degrees for several hours and that's no laughing matter as far as body temperature is concerned. If you have a high fever for a long period of time it can cause brain damage or worse and that's got me scared. He's sleeping right now, but just recently he had these crazy hallucinations and what I'm guessing was a seizure.

I feel like I'm in some kind of horror film. I mean, the things Wyatt's been saying for the past few hours make absolutely no sense. Just a little while ago he was having a conversation with our grandfather . . . and he's been dead for five years! It's like he's channeling the spirits or something. Then he freaked out thinking there were spiders crawling all over him, but there weren't. I've never seen anything like it and I thought that he was losing his mind so I shook him and squeezed his arm and tried desperately to wake him from this weird dream state or whatever he was in, but he wouldn't come to no matter what I did. It was like he was possessed.

As frightening as the hallucinations were, his seizure was downright horrifying. Out of nowhere his arms curled up and his neck muscles stiffened and he started making this awful noise like he was trying to clear his throat and he was twitching and his eyes started rolling back in his head.

"Stay with me, Wyatt!" I yelled. "Stay with me!"

In a panic, I ripped off my belt, folded it over, and shoved it between his teeth so he wouldn't bite off his tongue. Forcing his mouth open with the belt seemed to clear his airway and right away he took these big, gasping breaths and kind of relaxed and within a few minutes he had fallen into a deep sleep. It probably lasted ten or fifteen seconds, tops, but it seemed like a hundred years and scared me so bad, I literally thought I was going to have a heart attack just watching him.

Jubjub is trying to reach my parents in the Kalahari and even though the situation is really bad I asked her to please downplay the whole thing a little, otherwise they are going to flip and like I said, there's nothing they can do. She also radioed the hospital in Gaborone, but they can't send a helicopter until morning. Jubjub is on standby and will update the hospital with Wyatt's condition at 5:30 a.m. If he needs to be evacuated, they will send a chopper, which can be here within a couple hours, but I'm terrified he won't even make it to morning. I mean, his breathing is all over the place. Sometimes his breaths are short and quick. Other times he won't inhale for ten or fifteen seconds and whenever this happens I become terrified that I'm watching my brother die right before my eyes and it totally sends me into a panic and I hit him on the chest, smack his face, scream at him—anything to get him to breathe! Once he does, I collapse on the ground in relief.

It's just crazy the way an illness puts your feelings for someone in perspective. There are days when Wyatt aggravates me so much I swear I could kill him, but now that he's really in danger, I'd do anything to save him.

I can't help but regret leaving our parents in the Kalahari to join Chocs and Tcori on this expedition. It was a terrible, terrible decision.

## GANNON
4:47 AM

I've been up most of the night looking after Wyatt. He finally stopped fidgeting and calmed down a little while ago and slept. I've probably stuck my finger under his nose a thousand times to make sure he's still breathing. No joke, when he's just lying there all quiet and still, it looks like he's dead! This whole ordeal is incredibly stressful and has probably taken ten years off my life, but it looks like he recently made a turn for the better.

About an hour ago, his face became red and splotchy and beaded up with sweat and he went on sweating for a good stretch and then the sweat stopped and his face returned to a normal color. I felt his forehead and noticed it was much cooler. He was conscious for a few minutes and even able to answer questions with a simple nod or shake of the head. When I asked him if he felt any better, he actually nodded yes, which alone was a huge relief. Right now, he's sleeping again.

More later . . .

## GANNON

5:42 AM

Just before sunrise, Wyatt sat up and drank a half cup of tea and even said good morning when Chocs came into the tent. All these things may seem like really simple tasks, but they mark a gigantic improvement as far as Wyatt's concerned. After all, just a few hours ago the kid was so incoherent he could hardly speak, so things are definitely looking up. Right away, Chocs noticed that I was about to fall facedown in the dirt from exhaustion, so he relieved me of my watch and ordered that I get some rest—an order I will gladly obey.

# WYATT

AUGUST 27, 7:24 PM
OKAVANGO DELTA
15° CELSIUS, 59° FAHRENHEIT
SKIES CLOUDY, WIND 5-15 MPH

I write this journal entry seated beside a warm, crackling campfire. Writing takes a decent amount of mental energy, and I'm still feeling a little shaky, but the fact that I even want to write is proof that I am on the mend.

Yesterday when I started to feel bad, I got really worried and became desperate for something that would make me feel better, so I asked Tcori if the Bushmen had any natural remedies for a fever. Tcori assured me that they did and went about gathering roots and leaves from an assortment of shrubs. He boiled them all in a pot, put the steaming concoction inside my tent, and told me to take long, deep breaths. Other than clearing my nasal passages, I don't know that this remedy did me any good. In fact, my headache actually got worse, and I became nauseated. Whether this was a result of the treatment or not is impossible to know. Not wanting to discredit Tcori's traditional medicine or offend him in any way, I thanked him for going to such great lengths to help me.

After Tcori's treatment, I slept for a while and remember waking up from time to time, feeling as miserable as I've ever felt in my life. Just before sunrise my fever broke and I woke in a sweat, but I felt much better. Chocs radioed Jubjub and let her know that my condition had improved. He felt I was on the road to recovery but asked Jubjub to keep the medical evacuation helicopter on alert, just in case.

I may not be completely out of the woods, but all signs are good. In other words, I think I will live to see another day. At times I had my doubts. From what I've been told, so did everyone else.

When I was shivering inside my tent, I was reminded of *Missionary Travels in Southern Africa*, by Dr. David Livingstone, a book I read before our trip. In his journals he describes a seven-month expedition from the Zambezi River to the west coast of Africa. During this expedition his crew experienced no fewer than thirty-one cases of fever, and by the time they reached the coast, most of the men had severe dysentery. Many years later, Dr. Livingstone himself died on an expedition in Zambia from internal bleeding caused by malaria and dysentery.

I suppose I'm just lucky that my illness was somehow cured. What doesn't kill you makes you stronger, right? And I do feel stronger and plan to continue my research with a renewed spirit. As the famous naturalist Charles Darwin once wrote, "A man who dares to waste one hour of time has not discovered the value of life." I wouldn't be surprised if Mr. Darwin had jotted this down after being laid up in bed with the flu. That's the irony of illness. It gives you a whole new appreciation for life.

Let the journey continue . . .

# GANNON

"Jubjub to Father. Come in Father. How is Wyatt?"

This was the radio call that woke me up mid-afternoon.

"Hello, Jubjub," Chocs said. "He is doing much better. We plan to continue our search first thing tomorrow morning."

"That's wonderful news."

"You can notify the hospital that we won't be needing the helicopter. And please radio Wyatt's parents to let them know that he is okay."

"I will let everyone know right away!"

Boy, I can't even describe how relieved I was to hear this. Still totally wiped out from that awful experience, I stayed in my tent for a long time, just thinking about all the crazy stuff we've been through and enjoying the sound of everyone's voices outside. When I finally came out, it was time to make dinner. But first I had to give Wyatt a solid punch in the arm for putting me through that whole, ridiculous ordeal.

"It's good to see you, too," he said.

"Next time you pull something like that," I said, "I'm going to save myself the hassle and just feed you to the animals."

I was starving and helped gather sticks for a fire, stopping for a short time to watch a herd of elephants move slowly across the horizon. They even had a baby with them who stayed close as they all lumbered through the grasses under a big red sky.

Over dinner we discussed our plan and I was thinking for sure that Wyatt would vote to call off the expedition and return to Edo's Camp in the Kalahari. I mean, after being so sick it would have been totally understandable, but my brother is stubborn and wants to finish what we came to do.

So do I.

It's dark and I'm sitting by the campfire. Tcori just carved a bow and several arrows from the tree branches he collected and placed them above the fire to cure and then smiled at me and vanished into the darkness.

I think I should hit the sack. I slept for a while today, but it was mostly broken and coming off several nights of very little sleep, I'm still exhausted. I just can't seem to get my energy back. It's like it has been sucked right out of me. Last night really rattled my nerves. I'm hoping that after tonight I'll be all set with sleep and feel normal again. I'm hoping. In the morning, we resume our search.

## GANNON
AUGUST 28
7:47 AM

Okay, it seems totally ridiculous now, but one of the animals I was anxious to see in Africa was a baboon. I'm not really sure why. I guess it was just something about them, like the way they go about their business as if no one else on earth matters. Before our trip, I saw a video that was pretty hilarious of a family barbeque in South Africa being ambushed by a bunch of baboons. The family shouted and threw things, but the baboons were determined. They kept coming back and eventually ran off the humans and just started stuffing their faces with ribs and potato salad and rolls and chocolate pies. Here's something else I learned: Baboons don't waste food. Not a morsel. They ate every last thing and even licked the plates clean.

Of course, the delta is baboon country, so you'd think that someone who had seen how they can ransack a good picnic would take steps to stash their food away in a safe place before they went to bed for the night. But no, after rummaging around for a late-night snack I left our food container open and sitting outside my tent. Total idiot move, I know. Sure enough, just as I was falling asleep, I heard a ruckus outside my tent. I then made the mistake of sticking my head through the tent door and found myself face-to-face with the king of all baboons—if, in fact, baboons have kings.

Not knowing what else to do, I said something like, "Hey there, big fella." Well, he didn't like that too much and took a hard swipe at my face with his little human-looking baboon hand. Luckily he missed, and I quickly disappeared back into my tent.

I could kick myself. I mean, come on. Where's my brain? I broke one of the most basic rules of camping. You should always keep your food sealed in an animal-proof container, something that is airtight so animals can't pick up the scent. I guess I was just so tired I forgot to put the top back on. Chocs made me feel a little better this morning when he said, "You're lucky it was baboons that came for our food instead of hyenas. If it was hyenas, they would have eaten you, too."

Now, I'm going to have to agree with Chocs on that one.

Hyena on the hunt for its next meal, luckily it wasn't me

# WYATT

AUGUST 28, 8:01 AM
OKAVANGO DELTA
12° CELSIUS, 53° FAHRENHEIT
SKIES PARTLY CLOUDY, WIND 5-10 MPH

I was told Gannon probably saved my life the other night when I had a seizure, but this morning I could kill him with my bare hands! Thanks to the dinner party he threw for the baboons, our food supply has been seriously diminished. If we hope to continue our mission, we'll have to depend on Chocs and Tcori to find food on the delta. I'm hoping that won't be a problem, as Tcori has lived off the land his entire life. But it will definitely slow our search for the lioness, as some of our time will now have to be spent finding food. It's just one more obstacle we must overcome, but I suppose that's the nature of adventure.

## WYATT

AUGUST 28, 12:19 PM
OKAVANGO DELTA
26° CELSIUS, 79° FAHRENHEIT
GATHERING STORMS TO THE NORTH, WIND 15-20 MPH

As it turns out, the baboon debacle was not without its benefits. Since we had to clean up their mess, we were an hour or so behind schedule. If we'd left on time, it's likely that we would not have crossed paths with the Cape buffalos!

Saying that we "crossed paths" is really misleading. It would be more accurate to say that we were surrounded by them. Having just passed through a stretch of woods, we noticed a dust cloud up ahead. We climbed up a small dune for a closer look and saw a herd of Cape buffalos stretching across the plains as far as we could see. Chocs estimated there were at least 500 buffalos, and suddenly, every one of them was staring right at us! Intimidating, and that's putting it mildly.

My dad says Cape buffalos have a look that says, "Don't mess with me, sucker!" and he's right. They're known to be one of the toughest and most aggressive animals in Africa. They kill more than a few humans each year and can even put up a fight against a lion.

I quickly snapped a few photos. But as the herd moved closer, I decided to put away the camera. I thought the sound of the camera's shutter opening and closing might cause a stampede. At first, the herd was a little hesitant, but then they started to move around us. There was nowhere we could go, as this giant herd of buffalos stretched all the way across the horizon. We basically had to stand still and let them pass. As they did, one of the buffalos, a large male, took a few quick steps toward us and then stopped. It was as if he was reminding us that they were in charge. Not that we needed a reminder. We knew darn well.

Chocs and Tcori whispered to remain calm and not make any sudden movements.

"Cape buffalos are most aggressive when they are alone," Chocs said, without moving a muscle. "That's when predators take advantage and attack them. As a herd they feel safe, so they're not likely to harm us as long as we keep quiet."

Just then, Gannon whispered to Chocs.

"What if I feel a sneeze coming on?" he said.

"Do you feel one coming on?" Chocs asked.

"I think so."

"Try your best to hold it."

A tense standoff with a herd of Cape buffalos

"That's going to be difficult."

"Gannon," I said in a deadly serious tone, "I don't care if you have to hold your breath for the next ten minutes. You better not sneeze."

It's likely a normal sneeze may go unnoticed by such a large herd, but a Gannon sneeze, that's different. When Gannon sneezes it's like a Category 5 hurricane just blew ashore. He could literally blow the stink off a pig. I was afraid it would scare the buffalos half to death and get us all trampled. Gannon closed his eyes tight and plugged his nose with his fingers. His face turned bloodred, and veins bulged in his forehead. We all held our breath, fearing the worst.

It looked like his head was about to explode. Then all of a sudden, he dropped his hands and whispered calmly, "We're good. Sneeze went away."

The herd walked by at a leisurely pace. Some of the buffalos were so close their rough hides scratched us as they passed. With the exception of a few snorts here and there, they showed no signs of aggression. It was like they were out on a casual morning stroll, one buffalo blindly following another. Within ten minutes, they had all disappeared into the bush. About ten minutes after that, I finally stopped shaking.

## GANNON
DON'T KNOW THE DATE, OR TIME, FOR THAT MATTER

I've always thought of snakes as a slithery reptile that should be avoided at all costs, but today Tcori actually went in search of one.

We'd just stopped for a rest when he set off.

"Where is he going?" I asked Chocs.

"To find some lunch," he answered.

"What are we having for lunch?" I asked hesitantly.

"That depends on what he finds," Chocs answered. "Let's build a fire."

While we collected dry sticks for the fire, I watched Tcori, hoping that by some miracle he'd stumble upon something that would actually taste good. He was just walking around and looking up into the trees and bending down and peeking into all these holes and burrows. Chocs, Wyatt, and I were filling a shallow pit with our wood when I saw Tcori kneel down and poke a stick deep into one of the holes. When he stood up, a large, black snake slithered from the hole, obviously bothered by the stick that was being jammed into his home. The snake rose up like it was about to strike and I thought for sure that Tcori was in big trouble, but the poor reptile didn't have a chance. With the swipe of his stick, Tcori pinned the snake to the ground, held it steady, and chopped off its head with his spear. Even without a head, the body of the snake kept moving for a few seconds—curling up and slithering and flopping around—before it finally lay still in the dirt.

"Whoa," I said, surprised by what I had just seen. "That was pretty gruesome."

Tcori dragged the long body to us and tossed it near the fire pit. This snake was a monster, nine feet long, at least. Maybe ten.

"Gentlemen, lunch is served," Chocs said.

"I hope you're kidding," I said.

"No, I am not," Chocs replied with a smile.

"What kind of snake is it?" Wyatt asked.

"Black mamba," Chocs said.

"When we were in the Kalahari, Jubjub told us black mambas are poisonous," I said.

"Extremely poisonous."

"And we're going to eat it?" I asked, confused.

"Absolutely. The meat is delicious!"

Chocs explained that the venom is stored in a sack located in the back of the snake's head. As I mentioned, Tcori had already cut off the head, so, technically, the snake was safe to eat. Tcori took his knife and made an incision along the underbelly that ran the length of the snake. Then he took a firm hold of the scaly, black skin and started to tear it off, slowly exposing more and more of the snake's pinkish meat. For the final and most disgusting act of this performance, Tcori removed the guts with his hand and tossed them onto the ground near our feet.

I'm not going to lie. I almost puked.

As Tcori cooked the black mamba, its pasty meat crackling over the fire, I didn't think I'd be able to stomach a single bite. It was disgusting just to look at it, hanging there over the fire all pink and wormlike, but then again, it was my fault we were having to grill up poisonous snake in the first place, having given away our food to the baboons and all. So, it was snake or nothing and trekking through the bush you work up quite an appetite. I was beyond exhausted and literally starting to think that I might die if I didn't get some kind of nourishment.

By the time the snake meat was cooked, I was so hungry my stomach hurt. Tcori cut it into six-inch sections and handed a piece to each of us. The meat had turned golden brown and didn't look nearly as bad as it had when he first started cooking it. I'd never eaten snake, of course, so I set my portion on my lap and watched Tcori and Chocs peel strips of meat away from the bones and toss them into their mouths.

"Mmm," Chocs said. "Very good. Try it, Gannon and Wyatt. I think you'll like it."

Wyatt and I looked at each other, neither of us believing for a single second that we'd actually enjoy the taste of snake. I mean, if snake is so good, then why don't restaurants serve dishes like Teriyaki Python or Barbeque Rattlesnake? Reluctantly, I peeled a small strip of meat and quickly threw it into my mouth. Hard to believe, but it actually tasted decent. Okay, fine, I'll confess. Chocs was right. The snake was delicious.

"It tastes a lot like chicken," I said.

After swallowing his first bite, Wyatt agreed.

"Not bad," he said. "Not bad at all."

"Did you doubt me?" Chocs asked.

"Of course we doubted you," I said, and we all laughed.

I think our enjoyment of the black mamba probably had a lot to do with the fact that we were all so hungry the bark of a baobab tree would have tasted good.

All right, well, at least my belly's full now, and that's good because it's time to get going. Some nasty thunderclouds are gathering in the sky and it's important that we make some ground before the weather turns bad.

# WYATT

The rain has made it very difficult to trek any farther today and impossible to track the lioness. This is unfortunate because we were close. Just as the thunder began to rumble and clouds darkened overhead, we heard a roar in the distance. It was clear by our smiles that we were all thinking the same thing: *"That's her!"*

But just then the skies opened up and we experienced a downpour that would have sent Noah running for his ark. Not having an ark, we ran for some trees along a dried riverbed and quickly put up a tarp for shelter. Water soon flowed in the riverbed, turning the hill where we sat into a small island.

"This will be a good place to stay the night," Chocs said. "We're high enough from the water that our camp won't flood. And like the red lechwe, we can use the water to warn us of approaching predators."

I asked Chocs to explain.

"Red lechwes are a species of antelope," said Chocs. "They like to gather on islands and use the water as a warning system. As predators close in, the lechwes hear them splashing and know that danger is approaching. Lechwes are very fast in shallow water and can outrun the predator if they get a good head start. On dry land, they might not hear the predator until it's too late."

"Where's the safest place to stay when you're trekking in the African bush?" I asked. "On an island? In a tree? On the open plain?"

"In a hotel, if you can find one," Chocs said, followed by that great laugh of his.

A red lechwe on alert for predators

# GANNON

This morning I was sleeping like a rock and having this really awesome dream where I was on a sailboat in the middle of the ocean—which, if I had to guess, was probably brought on by the fact that we're camped on this little bump of land surrounded by water—when Chocs came into my tent and woke me up.

"Gannon," he whispered. "Come out of your tent and do it quietly."

"What now?" I thought. "Are we surrounded by a pod of hungry hippos?"

I put on my boots and crawled out my tent door, trying my best not to make any noise. Wyatt, Chocs and Tcori were looking up into the tree that spread out over our camp. About fifty feet above our heads was one of the most elusive creatures on earth, the leopard. Chocs later explained that leopards have sharp vision and radar-like hearing and typically flee when humans get too close and because of this it's very rare to see one, so we were lucky. This beautiful cat seemed totally comfortable around us, though, and went about its business of grooming its spotted coat with its long, pink tongue. Still, it was nerve-racking to know that there was a big cat sitting in a tree just over our heads that could jump down in about a second flat and kill us.

Tcori spoke, and Chocs translated. "This leopard has eaten

recently," Chocs said. "You can still see the blood around its mouth. As long as we don't do anything to make the leopard feel that it is in danger, we'll be okay."

We slowly packed up camp without saying much of anything to one another. The leopard was watching us, studying our every move. Once I was all packed up, I grabbed my camera to take some video, but when I looked back up into the tree, the leopard was gone.

"Oh, man, where did it go?" I whispered. Suddenly, I got this eerie feeling that it was about to leap onto my back and I kept turning around to make sure it wasn't sneaking up on me and ended up spinning around in circles so many times that I started to get dizzy. The leopard stayed hidden. We couldn't find it anywhere. Like a phantom in the night, it had completely vanished.

About fifteen minutes later, we were all packed and ready to start the day's trek, when I spotted the leopard. He hadn't disappeared after all. He'd just moved without making a sound.

"Wyatt," I whispered. "Turn around slowly. He's right behind you."

Just across the shallow riverbed sat the leopard, licking his paw under the shade of a tree like he didn't have a care in the world. Little rays of light were coming through the leaves. It was amazing the way the light made the leopard's eyes glow. I sat down and balanced my video camera on my knee to keep it steady while I filmed. Wyatt backed away slowly, got his camera ready and snapped off about a million photos. Eventually the leopard grew tired of all our gawking and picture taking. He stood up casually, gave a great yawn, and strolled away.

## WYATT

AUGUST 29, 6:51 PM
OKAVANGO DELTA
18° CELSIUS, 64° FAHRENHEIT
SKIES CLEAR, WIND 0-5 MPH
NUMBER OF PREDATORS IN A ONE-MILE RADIUS: TONS

As I write this journal entry, I am resting against the trunk of a tree, just happy to be in one piece. Our bravery was just put to the ultimate test, and to be honest, I nearly cracked under the pressure. I only hope that when all is said and done, we make it out of the bush alive. But we're beginning to push our luck.

There are countless stories of explorers dying in Africa. The most famous story of all, Dr. Livingstone, I've already mentioned. But the great Dr. Livingstone wasn't the only one. There are many others, such as Keith Johnston, the Scottish cartographer, who died of dysentery in the first weeks of his expedition to map the central lakes of Africa. Then there's Mungo Park, who was attacked by natives and drowned while attempting to chart the course of the Niger River. Another forty men on Park's expedition died from complications of malaria.

The list goes on—Clapperton, Lander, and Tuckey, just to name a few. We don't have to worry about bloodthirsty tribesmen these days, but there are other skillful killers that still wander these parts. Namely, lions.

When you are trekking through the bush, the high, golden grasses provide a perfect camouflage for lions. You could trip over a lion before you ever saw it. And today, we nearly did just that.

As the four of us were moving slowly across the delta, Tcori lifted his hand, signaling for us to stop. I watched curiously as he surveyed the area. It seemed like he detected something, but looking around I saw nothing out of the ordinary. Then, as if it appeared out of nowhere, a male lion rose up out of the grass just twenty feet from us.

When a lion is staring you in the face, your instinct tells you to turn and hightail it out of there as fast as you can. But I knew that running from a lion is hopeless. A human can't outrun a lion, and running will only encourage an attack.

The lion was disturbed and growled ferociously. Tcori took small steps backward and signaled us to do the same. But when we followed his lead, the lion grew even more aggressive and charged. Gannon was the closest to the lion, and it went right for him. Chocs quickly lifted his rifle and took aim. I held my breath and could hardly stand to watch. Just when I expected to see the lion leap at Gannon's throat, it stopped dead in its tracks. A mock charge, just as Chocs said lions often do. But that didn't mean we were safe. The lion was still agitated and considering its options. Attack or just back away? Chocs kept his finger on the trigger, ready to fire if the lion moved any closer.

Gannon remained perfectly still. How he kept his calm in the face of what seemed like certain death is beyond me. He was actually smiling at the lion, much like a dog owner smiles at his golden retriever. Maybe Gannon understood that his fate was in the hands of the lion, and there wasn't a thing he could do about it. Either that, or he was scared stupid. I'm going to guess the latter. But either way, he did exactly what he was supposed to do, and it saved his life.

Tcori waved his arm, attracting the lion's attention. When the lion turned to him, Gannon, Chocs, and I slowly backed away. Tcori spoke softly in his native language, and the lion followed him. When the lion moved uncomfortably close, Tcori would swat at it with the tip of his bow. This would send the lion scampering, but he was curious and kept coming back.

Tcori's bravery was nothing short of heroic. The fact that he would risk his own life to save ours, people he hardly knew, was very noble. I watched in awe as he continued to lure the lion away, until finally it lost interest and walked off, disappearing into the grass.

The male lion before he charged

# GANNON

Well, I totally blew it! I could have gotten the most amazing lion footage ever, but when that lion popped up out of the grass, I was so scared I couldn't even lift my arms, and when he ran at me, oh, jeez, I totally froze and my brain just shut down like a bolt of lightning had struck it and blown out all the circuitry. Maybe I was in shock. Who knows, but after the lion put on the brakes and was just standing there, looking at me, my brain started firing again, like the power had been restored, and I realized it had been a mock charge and I was just thinking, okay, kitty, don't worry about me, I'm no threat, look, I can't even move, good kitty, good kitty . . .

And what can I say about Tcori? The man faced down the king of beasts and saved my life. He's my hero!

Anyway, having just survived this whole crazy ordeal, I'm thinking the worst is behind us. I mean, it has to be! Then again, when you're in the bush, I guess you can never be certain of anything.

# PART III

## THE MOST DANGEROUS PREDATOR OF ALL

# GANNON
LATE AT NIGHT

Trekking through the delta, it's real easy to overlook the one species that's way more dangerous than a rhino or hippo or a leopard or even a lion. The species I'm talking about is humans.

As we came to the top of a bluff, Chocs spotted a small camp hidden in the forest.

"Stay low and move quietly," he said. "We're going in for a closer look."

My stomach was in knots as we crept through the bush like soldiers approaching an enemy encampment. Chocs was in the lead with his rifle drawn and cocked and ready for whatever we might encounter. It wasn't easy moving through that thick brush and my clothes kept getting caught in the bushes and my face and hands were getting all scraped up.

When we came to the edge of the bushes, we could see

the camp clearly just ahead of us. There was a green tarp stretched between two trees and a fire pit had been dug in the dirt and inside the pit, embers were still smoldering. Obviously, someone was in the camp, or very close by. Chocs ordered us all to get down on our stomachs and we waited for what seemed like years, just lying there in the dirt, watching for any sign of life. But we didn't see anything or anyone and I quietly hoped that Chocs and Tcori could take in all they needed to see from where we were and that we could get the heck out of there pronto, but, of course, that didn't happen. They decided that we should take a closer look around and told Wyatt and me to follow them.

There was a terrible stench in the camp, the stench of death. I pulled my shirt up over my nose it was so bad. There was no doubt about it: This was the poacher's camp!

We uncovered all kinds of awful things that had been hidden from view—there was a pile of elephant tusks buried under some brush and a leopard skin hidden in the shrubs, but most gruesome of all were the bloody rhino horns that Chocs discovered in a shallow pit. We had only one thing to be positive about. There were no dead lions, so we still had a chance to save the lioness and her cubs.

As I walked around camp, I couldn't help but think of the poor animals that had been killed by this evil person and wondered how in the world someone could do such a thing and I suddenly felt really, really sad, just thinking about these beautiful animals that had recently been roaming the delta with their families, free, the way they should be, and now they were dead. That kind of cruelty is just beyond me and the more I thought about it the more my sadness turned to anger. Something had to be done. This man needed to be punished for his terrible deeds and it was up to us to stop him before he killed again.

We knew we didn't have much time. The poacher could return at any moment, so we worked quickly to take down his camp. Wyatt went to work with his GPS and once he had the camp's coordinates, Chocs radioed them to Jubjub, who then sent the information to the authorities. Next we took all of the tusks, skins, and horns, loaded them onto a tarp and dragged them away from the camp. We purposely traveled over shrubs and grass, avoiding the sand so our footprints would be less obvious. It was hard work, and once we were about a quarter mile or so from camp we hid everything under a pile of shrubs. We decided that taking these things might keep the lions safe for a while because the poacher would obviously be irate when he found his camp ransacked and instead of hunting the lioness he would hunt the people who had taken his remains.

Just after we hid the last of the tusks, we saw a flashlight moving in the distance. We quickly shut off our own lights and took cover but apparently not soon enough. The poacher had spotted us and immediately opened fire. There was a rapid series of explosions. I dove to the ground and covered my ears. It was almost completely dark out, but the poacher's bullets were landing close. One even splintered a tree branch right next to me. I was terrified and buried my face in the dirt, trying to get as low to the ground as I possibly could. Bullets tore through the shrubs all around us. I thought we were goners for sure.

Chocs told us to follow him and stay low and we crawled on our stomachs through thick mud, slithering like snakes as bullets whizzed overhead. Just past a dune, the land sloped into a dry riverbed and we slid down the backside into a protected area where we could stand up and run for safety. One thing's for sure: I've never run so fast in my life! Fortunately, the poacher didn't follow.

We continued on through the brush and tried to stay low and navigate the dark without the use of our flashlights. We did this for what felt like several hours, the only help in our navigation being the pale light of the moon. Finally, we stopped for the night. We're hiding in a small clearing that's surrounded on all sides by thick bushes.

"Sorry, my friends," Chocs said, after we'd all collapsed on the ground from exhaustion. "No tents or campfire tonight. We must stay out of sight. It's likely that the poacher is tracking us. Try to get some sleep. We're moving out before sunrise."

It's safe to say that I will not sleep at all tonight. Don't know what time it is. Don't want to know. Just want morning to come. That's why I took out my journal in the first place, to pass time. Sitting in these bushes, most of the moonlight is blocked and I can hardly see what I'm writing, but aside from flicking away the bugs that are crawling all over me, there isn't a whole lot else to do.

I'm trying to keep my spirits up, and that's a tall order. Morale is definitely low. And we're hungry. My stomach growls just at the thought of food. Wyatt told me the human body can survive up to six weeks without eating, but I can hardly go six hours without feeling like I'm on the brink of starvation. I think I'll try to relax and focus on the sounds that echo through the bush at night. It's beautiful, the sound of Africa at night. The animals and insects create a natural symphony. So peaceful . . . if only we weren't being hunted by a poacher.

## WYATT
AUGUST 30, 7:28 AM
OKAVANGO DELTA, 19° 02' S 22° 44' E
9° CELSIUS, 48° FAHRENHEIT
SKIES CLEAR, WIND 10-15 MPH

Today is our seventh day in the bush. I did not expect it to take this long to find the wounded lioness and her cubs. Truthfully, I thought we'd track them down the first day. I don't think Chocs or Tcori anticipated such a long journey either. Of course, we could call off the search at any time and return to Shinde Camp, but that isn't really an option for me. We've been through too much to give up now.

Last night was long and I kept thinking I had a spider

crawling on me, and that just about drove me out of my mind. This morning as the sun was coming up, we picked some native fruits and nuts and rationed them between us. We'll have to hunt again today if we want to eat anything of substance. Maybe we'll get another snake, or possibly a guinea fowl, which is like a shiny blue chicken. It's important that we get some protein to keep up our strength.

I have taken our coordinates and calculated that we are approximately six miles southeast of the poacher's camp, which sits at 18°58′ S, 22°40′ E. We quietly radioed Jubjub again this morning, and I gave her our current location. She informed us that an anti-poaching unit had been assembled and will be traveling to the delta by helicopter soon. Anti-poachers are people who hunt down and arrest poachers. We can only hope that they arrive in time.

## GANNON

MID-MORNING
WYATT TELLS ME IT'S DAY #7, BUT I DON'T KNOW

We are taking a short break after an awfully long trek through thick brush. It was hard going in areas and we had to take turns clearing a trail with a machete. I need sleep. I'm starting to see things that aren't really there. Earlier, I thought a snake was slithering toward me, ready to strike, but it turned out to be nothing. It's crazy, the tricks your mind can play on you when you're tired. I'm on the verge of collapse, but there's no way I'm giving up.

# WYATT

AUGUST 30, 1:21 PM
OKAVANGO DELTA
25° CELSIUS, 77° FAHRENHEIT
SKIES CLEAR, WIND CALM

Oh, what a sight! Fresh lion and cub prints in the sand! Tcori said they were only hours old. The fact that the lioness hasn't bled to death already is a miracle. We must get to her immediately!

Lion prints in the sand

# GANNON

After spotting the lion prints, we followed them through the sand into another section of forest where the ground was covered with fallen leaves and twigs and soon after that we lost the trail. Or so I thought. Apparently Tcori could see something that we couldn't see because he kept moving like he was in a real hurry to get somewhere.

A few hundred yards into the forest, he turned to us and smiled. Sure enough, just ahead, lying near a termite mound, was the lioness and her four cubs. We didn't want to startle them, so we all took cover behind the trees. The lioness was lying flat on her side, panting heavily with all this blood smeared across her back hind leg. The poor thing looked like she was on the verge of death. The lion cubs didn't seem to have a clue that their mother was in such bad shape, as they continued to run around and wrestle playfully with one another in the leaves.

Tcori went right to work, smearing poison on the tip of one of his arrows. He then told us to stay put, and was creeping toward the lioness when one of the cubs, the runt of the litter, noticed Tcori and started jogging in his direction, probably thinking he wanted to play or something. Well, when the lioness saw the runt running away she got to her feet and her tail started to flip around and her ears went back, but she was just too weak to do much else. She could hardly even walk, and it was obvious she was in a lot of pain as she hobbled toward Tcori. Meanwhile, the little runt cub trotted right up to him, pawing at his leg like a house cat.

When Tcori was about fifty feet or so from the lioness, he drew back the arrow and let it fly. Man, does he have good aim. That arrow hit its mark dead-on, striking the lioness in the front right shoulder. She swatted it with her paw, and it fell to the ground, but the arrow had done its job, puncturing the skin and injecting the poison into her bloodstream. Tcori moved the runt toward its mother with his foot and once the cub had rejoined the others, Tcori backed off, keeping a close eye on the lioness the whole time.

"It will only be a little while before she is unconscious," Chocs said. "Once she is, we must work quickly to remove the bullet and stitch her wound. Gannon and Wyatt, your job is to occupy the cubs while we work. Remember, they may seem small and harmless, but they can give you a serious wound with their teeth and claws."

Then, like a flash, Tcori sprang to his feet and ran in the direction of the lioness.

"What's he doing?" I asked.

"Oh, no," Chocs said, pointing. "A cobra!"

Coiled up no more than ten feet from the lioness was a giant Egyptian cobra, one of the most venomous snakes in the world! Even a healthy lion would have trouble surviving a strike from one of these deadly reptiles. A weakened lion wouldn't stand a chance.

Tcori moved through the forest like an antelope running from a hyena, quickly putting himself between the cobra and the lioness. Right away, the cobra rose up higher and fanned its hood. The thing was ready to strike and we all held our breath knowing that one bite would mean the end of our friend, but Tcori remained calm, real calm, just standing there casually eyeballing the thing when suddenly, he thrust his arm at the snake with the speed of a lightning strike, grabbing it just under its hood. Obviously, the cobra wasn't so happy about this and fought like crazy to free itself, but Tcori had a solid hold, with his thumb pressed real hard under the snake's jaw so it couldn't strike. Wyatt and I looked on in complete awe of Tcori. The guy is totally fearless!

He carried the cobra far away from the lioness and her cubs and set it down at the base of a bush. Luckily, the snake slithered away without putting up any more of a fight.

## WYATT

AUGUST 30, 3:27 PM
OKAVANGO DELTA
28° CELSIUS, 82° FAHRENHEIT
SKIES CLEAR, WIND CALM

We got to the lioness just in time, but the clock was still ticking. After the lioness was unconscious, Chocs and Tcori went to work on her wound. It was fun to play with the cubs, but I was more interested in the surgical procedure involved in removing the bullet. So I left Gannon in charge of what he was calling "the lion-cub day care" and stood behind Chocs and Tcori to watch.

After sterilizing his hands with alcohol from the medical kit, Tcori dug into the wound with his fingers. He dug deeper and deeper until his hand was almost completely buried inside the lion. After some prodding, he found the bullet but couldn't get it out. It was lodged in a bone.

Then Chocs sterilized a pair of pliers and a hunting knife, and cut an incision on either side of the wound. This would give them better access to the bullet. He took the pliers and pushed them into the wound. After some maneuvering, he steadied his hand and squeezed. Sure enough, when he removed his hand from the lioness, there was a bullet pinched between the pliers.

Buzzing with excitement, I knelt down next to the lioness.

"You're going to be okay," I said, gently stroking the back of her head. "Everything is going to be just fine."

Suddenly, the lioness opened her eyes. My heart nearly stopped. Sitting next to an unconscious lion is one thing. Sitting next to a conscious lion is a different ball game altogether.

Chocs and Tcori continued to stitch the wound, unaware that the lioness had woken up.

"Hey," I whispered nervously. "Better wrap it up. She's awake."

Almost as an added warning, the lioness exposed her deadly canine teeth. She hadn't eaten in days, so it was reasonable to assume that these teeth would be tearing into some poor animal's flesh in the very near future. I just wanted to make sure it wasn't my flesh.

Chocs was just tying up the last stitch when the lioness lifted her head and roared. It was good to see that her strength was returning, but it also meant that we had to get moving on the double. I tossed Chocs and Tcori their packs and dragged Gannon away from the lion cubs.

"That went as well as it could have," Chocs said, as we made fast tracks through the bush. "She will be sore for a while, but I don't believe there was any permanent damage."

I couldn't imagine that the lioness would be able to chase and kill her prey until she was back to full strength, so I asked Chocs what she would do in the meantime to feed herself and her cubs.

"She will go after smaller animals until she is strong enough to bring down something bigger," Chocs explained. "Baby impala, warthogs, even birds. Lions are also scavengers, which means they take advantage of easy meals, like animals that die of natural causes. But I'm confident she'll be able to hunt at full strength again soon."

We have stopped for a much-needed rest. Other than some soreness in my legs, I'm feeling great. On top of the world! After all we've been through, we accomplished our mission. This is, without question, one of the proudest moments of my life.

## GANNON

Now, I'm no surgeon so I stayed out of that whole bullet-removal ordeal and looked after the mama's cubs while she was being tended to. I mean, puppies and kittens are cool and all, but playing with a lion cub beats playing with a dog or a cat any old day of the week.

The mother lioness and her cub

Goes without saying, but the cubs took a liking to me right away. They were jumping up on my legs, and clawing at me and wrestling one another for my attention. They may be small, but their teeth and claws are super sharp. I learned this the hard way, sticking my hand in one of the cub's mouths like I've done with puppies before, not really thinking it'd be any different, but when you're playing with lion cubs that's not a very smart thing to do. The lion cub didn't mean any harm when it bit my hand. They all just wanted to play, so that's what we did.

The runt of the litter was my favorite. He wouldn't leave my side. When I picked him up, he wagged his little tail and licked my chin with such excitement you would have thought it was covered in honey. I wanted so badly to take him home with me, but I knew that wouldn't be right. His family would miss him too much. And imagine trying to get a pet lion through airport security. Talk about a headache.

Okay, break time is over. We're all anxious to get back to Shinde Camp and we've got a long trek ahead. Sore feet don't fail me now.

## WYATT

AUGUST 30, 4:17 PM
OKAVANGO DELTA, 19° 08′ S 22° 46′ E
25° CELSIUS, 78° FAHRENHEIT
SKIES CLEAR, WIND CALM

We had been hiking for about a half hour, making good progress over grassy plains along the edge of a forest, when a gunshot stopped us dead in our tracks. Before we even had time to run for cover, the poacher stepped out from behind a bush.

His high-powered rifle was pointed directly at us. He wore a patch over his left eye. His right eye was black as night.

He approached slowly. "Drop the rifle, or I'll shoot!" he yelled.

Chocs did as he said.

"Everyone else put your hands up!"

The poacher moved quickly to Chocs, picked up the rifle and slung it over his shoulder. Without a weapon, we had no way of defending ourselves.

"We don't want any trouble," Chocs said.

"That's too bad, mate," the poacher responded. "Because you've got some."

"Why don't we each go our own way and pretend we never saw each other?" Chocs said.

"Too late for that," the poacher said. "You stole something of mine, and I'm here to take it back. So do yourself a favor, and tell me where I can find my tusks!"

We all stayed quiet, which only made the poacher angrier.

"Where are they?" he yelled. "I'm not going to ask again!"

Again, no one answered.

"So, you'd rather die, is that it?"

The poacher brought the rifle to his shoulder, lowered his head to the scope and took aim at Chocs.

"So be it," the poacher said.

"Wait!" I yelled. "Don't shoot! I have the coordinates! I wrote them down in my notebook. It's in my bag."

"Give that notebook to me," he said and turned his rifle on me.

I took off my backpack, set it on the ground and unzipped it. Pretending to rummage around inside the pack, I grabbed my GPS and quickly took our coordinates. My hands began to sweat. I knew that if the poacher discovered what I was doing, he would shoot me.

"Hurry up!" the poacher yelled. "I'm losing my patience!"

"I'm sorry," I said. "I have too much stuff in my backpack. It's almost impossible to find anything."

"Let's hope for your sake that you find it quickly!"

I knew I couldn't stall much longer. My hands were shaking as I typed an "SOS" message into the radio and sent it to Jubjub. I could only hope that she received it.

"If you don't find that notebook in ten seconds, I'll have you digging your own graves!"

"I found it!" I said, removing the notebook from my backpack. I opened it and turned to the page where I'd written the coordinates.

"Here you go," I said, showing it to the poacher. "This is where you'll find your tusks, horns, and skins. It's all there hidden under some brush."

The poacher yanked the notebook from my hands and looked at the coordinates.

"You're obviously skilled in wilderness travel," he said. "I want you to take me there."

"I'll take you there if you let the others go," I said.

"You think you're making the rules here, do ya mate? Well, guess what, you're not!"

"If you don't let them go, you'll never find your tusks."

The poacher thought for a minute. He then gathered all of our packs and dumped them out on the ground. Sorting through our equipment, he found the radio and immediately stomped it to pieces with his heel. He also found my GPS and was about to crush it with the butt of his rifle when I stopped him.

"Don't!" I said. "We need that to find our way!"

He stopped short, knelt down, and picked up the GPS.

"You better not be playing games with me, boy. If I find out you are, you're finished."

"I promise, I'm not."

He put the GPS in a satchel and then searched each of us to see if we had anything hidden in our pockets.

"If you have other radios or satellite phones, hand them over right now. I can't have you calling the authorities."

"You've seen everything we have," Chocs said. "We have no way to communicate with anyone."

"What's to prevent you from radioing once you reach camp?"

"We're at least ten hours from our camp," I said. "I'm guessing we'll find your tusks within a few hours, tops. You'll have time to collect your things and go on your way long before they even get back."

This information seemed to calm the poacher's nerves.

"The three of you stay put until we're out of sight," the poacher said. "Then you can be on your way." He then turned to me. "Let's get moving. It will be dark before long."

"No, wait!" Chocs said, moving toward the poacher. "Take me instead!"

The poacher turned his gun on Chocs.

"Take one more step, and it will be your last!"

Chocs froze.

"I'm taking the boy, and that's the last of it!"

There was nothing else Chocs could do. If he made another move, the poacher would kill him.

I nodded to Chocs to assure him that I would be okay. Truthfully, though, the thought of trekking through the delta at gunpoint had my stomach rumbling like an African thunderstorm. What was going to happen to me once we found the tusks, horns, and leopard skin? What reason would he have for keeping me alive? This was a man who had no problem killing. He did it for a living. We had interfered with his mission, and I was sure he wanted revenge.

"Once you are there," Chocs instructed, "climb to the top of the highest tree. You'll be less vulnerable to predators and easier for us to spot. Tcori and I know the delta like the back of our hands. As soon as we arrive at camp, we'll get a vehicle and come for you."

"Enough!" the poacher yelled, pressing the barrel of his rifle in my back. "Get going and keep your hands where I can see them! Try anything and believe me, you'll regret it!"

I looked at my brother, and couldn't help thinking that it might be the last time I ever see him.

"If you hurt him," Gannon said, "we'll find you."

"You worry about yourself, mate," the poacher said. "You have to cross the delta without a weapon. Chances are you'll be eaten alive before nightfall." He turned to me. "Now, go! We have no time to waste!"

The poacher shoved me hard in the back, and we began our march. My fate was sealed.

"Hang in there, Wyatt!" Gannon said. "We'll come for you!"

Just then I heard something in the distance. It almost sounded like a machine gun. As I turned around a helicopter suddenly rose up from behind the trees. I couldn't believe it. The anti-poachers had arrived!

## GANNON

Okay, just for the record, this has been one of the craziest, most action-packed, nerve-racking days I've ever had—and will probably ever have—well, with the lions, and the poacher and the anti-poachers and Wyatt being held at gunpoint. I mean, it took just about every ounce of stamina and courage we had just to get to the lioness and her cubs, but we did it and I thought it was all over, and then the poacher jumps out of nowhere and takes my brother hostage! I was thinking for sure Wyatt was a goner, that we were all goners, and then I saw the anti-poaching helicopter, and I'm like, thank heavens this nightmare is finally over! We're saved! I mean, there was nowhere for the poacher to run, so I assumed he'd throw down his gun and surrender, but unfortunately the poacher had other plans.

In a single nanosecond the poacher grabbed Wyatt around the neck and put a gun to his head. My heart jumped into my throat. The chopper landed nearby, and three men in military uniforms jumped out. They were armed with rifles and all of them were pointed at Wyatt and the poacher.

"No, don't shoot!" I screamed. "He has my brother!"

The poacher had him in a choke hold and Wyatt's face was turning bright red. He fought as hard as he could to loosen his grip, but the poacher was much bigger and kept his arm locked tightly around Wyatt's neck.

"Come one step closer, and I'll put a bullet in this kid!" the poacher yelled.

The anti-poachers stopped but kept their guns aimed at the poacher. Wyatt gasped for breath.

"Everyone put your guns down, and do it slowly!" the poacher continued.

They did as he said, laying their guns on the ground. He then motioned to the pilot to keep the helicopter running.

"Now everyone turn around and lie on the ground! I'm taking the helicopter and if anyone tries to stop me, the kid's as good as dead!"

With my legs trembling, I turned around and knelt

down slowly. Just as my knee hit the dirt, a shot rang out. I spun around, horrified by what I might see. The poacher let out a scream, staggered, and fell backward, gripping his thigh with both hands. Blood soaked his pants. He'd been shot in the leg!

I looked around frantically to see where the shot had come from. Jumping from the helicopter was a fourth man in camouflage. He had been hiding behind the seats and held a smoking rifle in his hands.

The other three men grabbed their rifles and ran to the poacher.

Chocs, Tcori, and I ran to Wyatt as fast as we could. He was so shaken that he had fallen to the ground and could hardly breathe.

"Relax," Chocs said. "It's all over."

I helped Wyatt to his feet.

"I thought you were dead," I said.

"So did I," Wyatt said, his voice faint and unsteady.

"I knew that guy was up to no good when I saw him in Maun," I said, referring to the poacher. "I could tell by looking at him that he was evil. He had the eye of a vulture."

The men showed the poacher no sympathy as they tied his hands behind his back and dragged him across the ground to the helicopter.

The man who shot the poacher walked up and introduced himself.

"I'm General Mozello," he said. "We've been looking for

you. When we got the SOS call from Jubjub, we knew where to find you and came immediately."

"Your timing couldn't have been better," I said.

"I wonder how Jubjub knew we were in trouble?" Chocs asked.

"I sent her an SOS before the poacher took all of our gear," Wyatt said.

"That was quick thinking, Wyatt. And very brave of you."

"Credit goes to Jubjub for acting on it. I guess she really is a *savior.*"

"It seems so," Chocs said with a smile.

"General, that was an incredible shot," Wyatt said. "Please tell me it wasn't just luck that you hit him and not me."

"I am a professional sharpshooter," said the general, with a smile. "I can shoot a feather off an eagle from a mile away . . . while it's flying."

He probably wasn't joking.

"I don't know what else to say, but thank you. You saved my life."

"Glad I could be of service. A second helicopter will be arriving shortly to take you back to camp."

We watched as General Mozello's men shoved the poacher into the helicopter. He fought and squirmed to break free, but it was useless, as one of the larger anti-poachers had him pinned hard to the floor. As the helicopter lifted off, he stared eerily at us with that dark, sinister eye. I'm sure he was wondering how a couple of kids managed to help thwart his poaching operation, but I suppose he'll have plenty of time to figure that out in jail.

## WYATT

AUGUST 30, 8:07 PM
OKAVANGO DELTA
19° CELSIUS, 67° FAHRENHEIT
SKIES CLEAR, WIND CALM

My parents were waiting anxiously when our helicopter landed at Shinde Camp, as was Jubjub, who ran over and hugged her dad and wouldn't let go.

"Oh, it's so good to see you boys," my mom said, tears welling up in her eyes.

"You have no idea how worried we've been," my dad said. "Mom started to think you weren't going to make it back alive."

"We thought the same thing a time or two," Gannon said.

"Or three," I added.

"I haven't been able to sleep since we got word that Wyatt was sick," my mom said. "There were no planes available in the Kalahari for several days, so we drove twelve hours on a safari bus to get here. Some of the Bushmen came with us to make sure Tcori was okay."

"Tell us what happened," my dad said. "We're dying to know."

"Wyatt fought off a croc attack," Gannon blurted out with a sly grin.

I just glared at him.

"Is that true?" my mom asked.

"No," I said. "Gannon is just trying to be funny."

"Did you find the lioness?" my dad asked.

"We did," I said. "And she's going to be fine."

"That's great news! What about the poacher?"

"He got shot," Gannon said matter-of-factly.

My mom gasped and covered her mouth with her hands.

"Is he dead?" she asked in horror.

"No, but he'll probably walk with a limp the rest of his life."

"I can't believe it," my dad said, rubbing his head. "You boys are lucky to be alive. If I'd known you were going to be in danger, I would have never let you go."

He paced back and forth.

"What kind of parents are we to send our kids into the African bush when there's a poacher in the area? I don't know what we were thinking!"

"We accomplished our mission and made it back safe," Gannon said. "That's all that matters."

"Part of me doesn't want to hear any more of these stories," my dad said, "but curiosity is going to get the best of me sooner or later. So tell us more about this adventure of yours."

"You can read all about it in my journal," I said. "I've got everything documented."

"So do I," Gannon said, handing his journal to our mom.

"That's good," my mom said, "because your English grades depend on it."

For the first time in what seemed like forever, we all laughed.

"You can read them after dinner," I said. "First things first, we need something to eat."

"Yeah, what's for dinner?" Gannon asked. "We haven't had a square meal since the baboons invaded our camp and ate all our food."

"Baboons ate your food?" my dad asked. "Unbelievable! I've got to hear this."

"Read our journals."

"All right, all right. We've got some kudu steaks on the grill. They should be ready soon."

"Your sons are brave young men," Chocs said. "You should be very proud."

"We are," my mom said. "They're always up for an adventure."

"They are true explorers," Chocs said. "If Dr. Livingstone were alive today, I don't think he could find two boys better suited for an African expedition than Gannon and Wyatt."

## GANNON

After dinner we met several members of Tcori's family. They had come along with my parents on the safari bus and were relieved to find Tcori safe and sound. As the sky grew dark and the moon rose under the shimmering stars and the air took on a chill, the Bushmen lit a campfire—big and warm and crackling with flames that reached up at the sky—and we all gathered in the red glow of this small inferno and celebrated with traditional song and dance. I grabbed my camera and recorded everyone clapping and cheering and stomping around the fire, but again I couldn't resist and eventually found myself dancing right alongside the Bushmen. Not wanting to be outdone by his twin brother, Wyatt brought his awkward moves to the party, looking a lot like a kid who'd woken up with a really stiff neck. Even my parents joined the dance. At least now I know where Wyatt learned his moves.

The Bushmen celebrate our safe return

We really couldn't have asked for a better way to end our first African adventure, and I say first for a reason. I am forever changed at having experienced this incredible place, and we've only scratched the surface. Just as so many great explorers returned to this beautiful and mysterious continent again and again, so, too, will we.

*Until next time . . .*

# GANNON & WYATT's

The Alaskan Arctic

North Pole

Baffin Island

Denali

Kodiak Island

Cliffs of Moher, Ireland

Great Bear Rainforest

Yellowstone Park

Niagara Falls

Stonehen

Moab    Badlands

Paris, Fran

Grand Canyon

New Orleans

Barcelona, S

Everglades

Tropic of Cancer

Bermuda Triangle

Casablanca, Mor

The Caribbean

Big Island, Hawaii

Galapagos Islands

The Amazon River

Machu Picchu, Peru

Tropic of Capricorn

Patagonia

# TRAVEL MAP

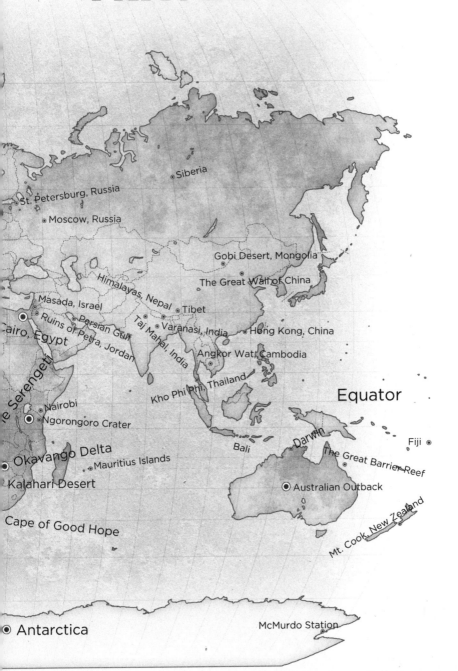

Siberia

St. Petersburg, Russia

Moscow, Russia

Gobi Desert, Mongolia

The Great Wall of China

Himalayas, Nepal

Masada, Israel · Tibet

Ruins of Petra, Jordan · Persian Gulf

Cairo, Egypt

Taj Mahal, India · Varanasi, India · Hong Kong, China

Angkor Wat, Cambodia

The Serengeti

Kho Phi Phi, Thailand

Equator

Nairobi

Ngorongoro Crater

Bali · Darwin

Fiji

Okavango Delta

Mauritius Islands

The Great Barrier Reef

Kalahari Desert

Australian Outback

Cape of Good Hope

Mt. Cook, New Zealand

Antarctica

McMurdo Station

# AUTHORS' NOTE

When we travel, either physically or vicariously through a book or film, we cannot help but be awed by the incredible diversity of our planet. Traveling opens our minds to different ways of thinking and introduces us to different ways of being. Travel presents us with possibilities we may have never considered.

However, the earth is losing its diversity at an alarming rate. Scientists estimate that since 1970 as much as a third of the world's wildlife has been lost. Ancient cultures and languages are disappearing as well, and with them thousands of years of wisdom. These cultures have different ways of perceiving life and our connection with nature. In times of rapid global change, such knowledge is more important than ever. In fact, it may offer solutions to some of our greatest challenges.

By introducing young people to different cultures and environments through storytelling, we hope to plant a seed that will inspire the preservation of biological and cultural diversity on our planet. Two of the last great places we can find such diversity are the Kalahari Desert and Okavango Delta of Botswana. As with any area rich in resources, the Kalahari and Okavango face threats. Poaching, loss of habitat, and human development place pressure on the ecosystem. In the decades to come, younger generations will play a critical role in the fate of such places and the well-being of the planet as a whole. The sooner young people take an interest, the greater the chances that the earth's wondrous diversity will be preserved for generations to come.

Gannon and Wyatt in the Okavango Delta, Botswana

## MEET THE "REAL-LIFE" GANNON AND WYATT

Have you ever imagined traveling the world over? Fifteen-year-old twin brothers Gannon and Wyatt have done just that. With a flight attendant for a mom and an international businessman for a dad, the spirit of adventure has been nurtured in them since they were very young. When they got older, the globe-trotting brothers had an idea—why not share with other kids all of the amazing things they've learned during their travels? The result is the book series, Travels with Gannon & Wyatt, a video web series, blog, photographs from all over the world, and much more. Furthering their mission, the brothers also founded the Youth Exploration Society (Y.E.S.), an organization of young people who are passionate about making the world a better place. Each Travels with Gannon & Wyatt book is loosely based on real-life travels. Gannon and Wyatt have actually been to Botswana and tracked rhinos on foot. They have traveled to the Great Bear Rainforest in search of the mythical spirit bear, and explored the ancient tombs of Egypt. During these "research missions," the authors, along with Gannon and Wyatt, often sit around the campfire collaborating on an adventure tale that sets two young explorers on a quest for the kind of knowledge you can't get from a textbook. We hope you enjoy the novels that were inspired by these fireside chats. As Gannon and Wyatt like to say, "The world is our classroom, and we're bringing you along."

## HAPPY TRAVELS!

Want to become a member of the
**Youth Exploration Society**
just like Gannon and Wyatt?

Check out our website. That's where you'll learn how to become a member of the Youth Exploration Society, an organization of young people, like yourself, who love to travel and are interested in world geography, cultures, and wildlife.

**The website also includes:**

Information about Botswana, amazing photos of the Kalahari and Okavango Delta, and complete episodes of our award-winning web series shot on location with Gannon and Wyatt!

## BE SURE TO CHECK IT OUT!
## WWW.GANNONANDWYATT.COM

# ACKNOWLEDGMENTS

We are forever grateful to Doug and Nancy Van Howd for introducing us to the magic of Africa; the Naru people for inviting us into their village and introducing us to the customs of the Kalahari Bushmen; and to John, Sue, Nigel, and Jo Kingsley-Heath for providing what we believe is the best adventure safari on the continent. We'd also like to offer a heartfelt thanks to Tom Wheeler and Heidi Hemstreet for your love, support, and encouragement. We cannot say enough about our wonderful editor, Catherine Frank, and the phenomenal team at Greenleaf Book Group Press. Thank you one and all! And, as always, thank you Gannon and Wyatt for your imaginative contribution to our fireside chats where our African adventure tale was brought to life.

# ABOUT THE AUTHORS

**PATTI WHEELER**, producer of the web series Travels with Gannon & Wyatt: Off the Beaten Path, began traveling at a young age and has nurtured the spirit of adventure in her family ever since. For years it has been her goal to create children's books that instill the spirit of adventure in young people. The Youth Exploration Society and Travels with Gannon & Wyatt are the realization of her dream.

**KEITH HEMSTREET** is a writer, producer, and cofounder of the Youth Exploration Society. He attended Florida State University and completed his graduate studies at Appalachian State University. He lives in Aspen, Colorado, with his wife and three daughters.

Ancient African Currency

# MY JOURNAL NOTES

_____

_____

_____

_____

_____

_____

_____

_____

_____

_____

_____

_____

_____

_____

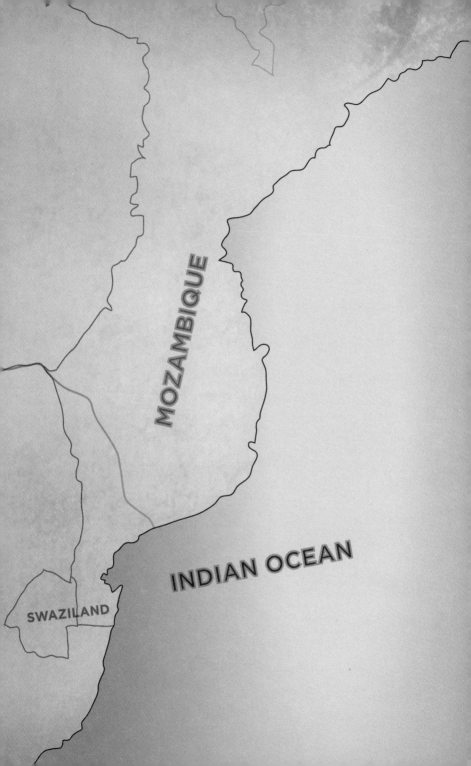

MOZAMBIQUE

INDIAN OCEAN

SWAZILAND

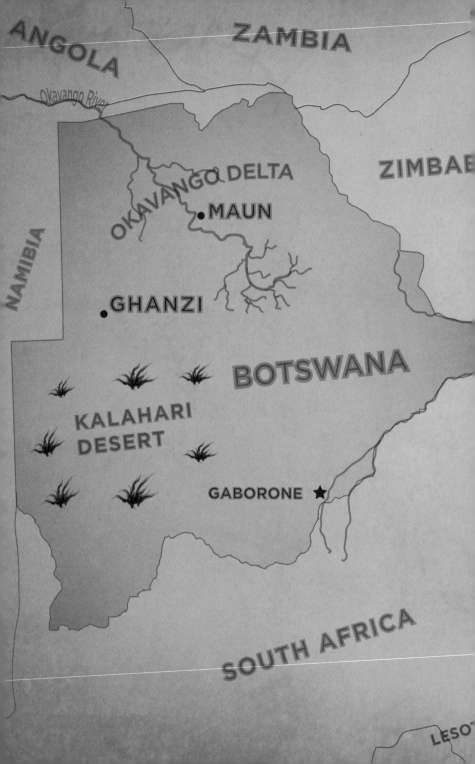